365 Animal Tales

OM
Om Books International

First Published in 2007 by

Om Books International
4379/4B Prakash House Ansari Road Darya Ganj
New Delhi 110002. India.
Tel: 91-11-23263363, 23265303
Fax: 91-11-23278091
Email: sales@ombooks.com
Website: www.ombooks.com

Reprint : 2009

ISBN: 978-81-87107-52-1

365 Animal Tales

Contents

The Story of the Month: The Wise Old Bird

The Story of the Month

The Wise Old Bird

01 The Wise Old Bird

There lived a flock of wild geese in a very tall tree. The tree was in a dense forest in the foothills of the Himalayas. The tall tree had many leafy branches that spread out like strong arms. Among the geese was an old wise bird who noticed that there was a small creeper growing at the foot of the tree. He showed the creeper to the others and said, "We must destroy it. One day it will grow big and then the hunters can easily climb up and kill us." But the other birds did not pay heed to his advice. They said it would be a pity to cut a small creeper. "But when it grows up, it will become strong and hard to cut," the old wise bird said. "We'll see," said the others and promptly forgot all about it.

As time passed, the creeper grew taller and stronger and winded its way up the tree just as the old goose had once said. One day when the geese had gone out

in search of food, a hunter climbed up the tree with the help of the creeper and laid his net there. In the evening when the geese returned, they found themselves trapped in the net, much to their shock. They tried hard to get out but failed. They cried for help but there was no one to hear their cries. The night passed in fear and worry. The old wise bird said, "I had warned you all to cut off the creeper but you did not listen. This is the result of your own folly. Tomorrow morning the hunter will come and kill us all." The birds realised that they had been foolish in not listening to the wise bird and said they were sorry. They had learnt a big lesson. Then the wise bird said, "I'll tell you of a plan to escape. Listen carefully. Tomorrow morning when the hunter comes to take his net, be very still and pretend you are dead. He will not want dead birds so he will throw us to the ground. Before he climbs down, we must all quickly fly away. That is the only way we can escape now."

The geese waited eagerly for the morning to arrive. The hunter came early next morning with his son. He was glad to see that he had caught so many geese. But when he climbed up the creeper, he saw that they were all dead. So, he threw the geese to the ground one by one while his son watched.

Whoosh! All the geese flapped up in the air and flew away. The hunter and his son were left staring after the geese, shocked and puzzled by the sight.

02 The Monkey's Heart

Once upon a time there was a clever monkey who lived by the river Ganga. A crocodile and his wife lived in the same river. One day, the crocodile's wife fell very ill. She wanted to eat something special. She asked her husband to get her a monkey's heart. The crocodile did not know what to do. Then he thought of his neighbour, the monkey. He said, "Friend Monkey, why do you waste your time eating the fruits of this tree? There are juicy fruits on the other side of the river." When the monkey said that the river was too big for him to cross, the crocodile offered to take him on his back. After a while, the crocodile sank in the water along with the monkey. He told the monkey that his wife was sick and wanted his heart. The monkey realised that he had been foolish to trust the crocodile. He quickly thought of a clever plan to escape. He said, "Alas friend! Our hearts are not inside us. We have to keep them hanging on trees. I wish you had told me earlier. Let's go back and bring my heart." The crocodile believed the monkey and brought him back to the tree. The monkey at once climbed up the tree and escaped. He said to the crocodile, "You have a big body but no brains!" The crocodile had nothing to do but repent for his foolishness on being tricked by the monkey.

03 The Tiger and the Woodpecker

Once as a tiger was eating, a bone got stuck in his teeth. He tried hard to remove the bone. A woodpecker saw the tiger's discomfort and asked what the matter was. The tiger pointed to his teeth. The woodpecker promised to remove the bone from his teeth on the condition that the tiger would always give him a portion of his food. The tiger agreed and the woodpecker took out the bone with its sharp beak.

One day, the tiger was eating and the woodpecker asked for a share. The tiger refused and said, "You should be thankful that I did not kill you when you entered my mouth." The woodpecker was enraged at the ungrateful tiger. He pecked the tiger in one eye. The tiger roared with pain and the woodpecker said, "You should be thankful that I didn't blind both your eyes."

04 The Goat and the Ass

A man once owned two animals, a goat and an ass. The goat envied the ass because the ass could eat a lot of food.

One day, the goat said to the ass, "I pity you! One moment you have to work in the mill and the next moment you have to carry heavy burden on your back. Why don't you fall down in the ditch and pretend to be ill? That way you can rest for some time."

The silly ass did just that. But he was badly hurt after falling in the ditch. His master called a doctor who advised that a goat's lungs should be rubbed on the ass's wounds. The farmer killed the goat to heal the ass.

Thus by wrongly advising the ass, the goat brought about his own death. You should never be jealous of other people.

05 Donald the Cat

A group of mice used to plunder Mr. Stewart's confectionery every night. There would be broken dishes, scattered trays and crumbs of food on the floor. The only one to rid him of the menacing mice, he thought, would be his cat, Donald.

Donald was a silly cat. He crept up quietly and pounced on them. All the mice ran for their life, except for one who got stuck in a bowl of pudding. When he saw Donald approaching, he took some cherries from the pudding and aimed them at the cat's eyes. As the cherries hit his eyes, Donald mewed for help and out popped all the mice. They sprayed chocolate sauce on Donald, threw breadcrumbs at him and chewed his tail. When Mr. Stewart arrived and saw Donald's condition, he cried, "Oh, you good for nothing fellow, you're a disgrace!" and shooed him away.

06 The Eagle and the Fox

Once an eagle and a fox were very close friends. "Let's live close to each other," they decided. So, the eagle built its nest on a tree while the fox lived in the bushes close by. One day, the fox went hunting. The eagle did not have anything to feed her eaglets. "I will get one fox cub," she thought and fed it to her young ones. When the fox returned, she was heartbroken. "You cheated me," she said in anger and sadness.

Soon God punished the eagle. One day, the eagle picked up a piece of goat flesh that the villagers had killed as a sacrifice, for her eaglets. She did not know that she was carrying a burning cinder along. The cinder set the nest on fire. The poor little eaglets got hurt. While the eagle cried, the fox said, "God has punished you for breaking a friend's trust."

07 The Fox and the Lapp

Once upon a time there was a cunning fox. One day, he lay in his cave feeling bored.

Suddenly he heard an approaching sledge. "Let me try out a trick," he thought. He then lay on the road, pretending to be dead.

Soon a Laplander passed by and saw the fox. "Oh! I will take this dead fox to the market," decided the Laplander and put the fox on his sledge. After some time, the Laplander found the fox lying on the road again. "How is this possible? I had put this fox in my sledge. It must be bewitched. I will put it in the other sledge," thought the Laplander and placed the fox in the sledge full of dead fish. The sly fox picked up a bagful of fish and slipped into the jungle. After some time the Laplander realised something was wrong, but he was too late. The fox had already taken his fish!

08 The Birdbath

A little girl called Megan had a birdbath in her backyard. Every day she would fill it with fresh water and many birds would come flocking to wash their wings and tails. One day Megan's friend, Gina came over. "Let's go and play," she said, "you can fill the bird-bath later." Megan hesitated but Gina was in such a hurry that she agreed. Since there was no water, the birds were disappointed and flew away. When Megan came back, her father showed her a lone blue bird that had been wait-ing all day. "That bird is also your friend, Megan. You have to think about her too," he said. Megan filled the birdbath and the blue bird splashed happily in it. To Megan's delight, all the birds were back the next day.

09 The Greedy Dragon

Once, in a big castle, there lived four little mice. Boret was the eldest while Yoba was the youngest. Daily, traders brought loaves of bread, nuts, and cheese to the castle. "I am the oldest so I will get the biggest piece!" declared Boret. Jilma and Hargon came next. "I never get anything!" wailed Yoba. One day, no trader came. "A big dragon is blocking their path," panted Squiggly the squirrel. Boret said, "What shall we do? We have to find a way out." Yoba replied, "I have an idea, but if it is successful then you must promise me that you will always divide the food equally." All of them agreed. The mice collected many jars of jam and took them to the dragon's cave. The dragon ate them all and had a terrible stomach ache. He clutched his stomach and groaned, "Oh, I am dying." The mice were hiding nearby. Yoba shouted from the hideout, "If you go to the mountains, you will never have a stomach ache again." The dragon believed them and went away. The traders began coming again and the mice were very happy.

10   The Cunning Rat

Jim was a cunning rat. One day, when he was just about to come out of his hole, he saw a cat waiting outside, ready to attack him. "If I go out now she will surely eat me up," thought Jim. He went back inside his hole and joined the other rats inside. There, he asked another rat, "Friend, why don't you come out with me to the cornfields? It would be nice to have your company." The second rat was simple and did not suspect anything. He agreed to accompany him. 'Yes, I would love to go with you. I've heard the field is full of goodies," he said. Then Jim said, "You are my guest. You must go first." So off they went, merrily hopping along. As soon as the other rat jumped out of the hole, the cat grabbed it and made a meal of it. Cunning Jim quickly raced past the cat without being noticed.

11   The Fox and the Bramble

Peter Fox was a grumpy and selfish fox. One day, he saw some kids gamboling alone in a field across a hedge. "They will make such a delicious meal," he thought, his mouth watering. He was climbing up the hedge, when suddenly, he slipped and was about to fall. He quickly clutched a thorny bramble to save himself. "Ouch! Ooooh! Help!" exclaimed the fox in pain. The bramble had pricked the fox all over and hurt him badly. He rubbed his sore body unhappily.

The fox became angry and said to the bramble, "I held on to you for help but you pricked me! I wish I had fallen on the hedge instead. The hedge wouldn't have hurt me this badly!" The bramble replied, "You are so selfish! I saved you from falling. Instead of thanking me, all you can think of are the tiny pricks you got! To the selfish, the whole world seems selfish!"

12 A Swaying Good Time

Bobo the monkey climbed a coconut tree. Soon the breeze began to blow a little stronger and the tree swayed from side to side. The coconuts started falling to the ground. Bobo held onto a coconut so that he would not fall. But there was sudden gush of wind and he fell down with a loud thud. More coconuts fell and hit Bobo on the head. Bobo thought it might be fun to hold the trunk and sway along with it. So that's what he did. "Whee!" he said and had a swaying good time! Then he fell for the second time. This time Bobo found a cave and rested there till the storm was over.

13 The Frog Girl

Once, there lived a poor childless couple. They longed for a child. After many years, the woman gave birth to a baby. But to their astonishment, instead of a normal human child, it was a girl frog! The couple raised their frog child with as much love as they would have given a normal child. She grew up to be an excellent singer. One day, a prince was passing by. Enchanted by her voice he exclaimed, "What a lovely voice! I wish to marry the owner of this melodious voice." Little did he know that the singer was actually a frog! The frog girl agreed to marry the prince on one condition. "I will enter the palace and bridal chamber in an enclosed carriage," she said. The prince agreed and they were married. At night, the frog hopped on to the bed but the prince pushed it away in disgust. The poor frog girl was heartbroken and went back home. Days passed. One day the prince once again passed by her house and heard her singing. He again wanted to marry the singer. This time the frog girl agreed to marry him without any condition. She sat in a little carriage that was pulled by a rooster. On the way, the prince met three fairies who gifted him with a fine horse carriage and many servants. The third fairy turned the frog girl into a beautiful maiden. After that, the maiden and the prince lived happily ever after.

14 The Bunny Family

Once upon a time there lived a Papa and Mama Bunny. They had four children—Angora, Harlequin, Lilac and little Rex. Papa Bunny loved working in his vegetable garden and grew all kinds of vegetables. One day, Papa Bunny went home for lunch. Angora hugged him, "Papa, did you bring a cabbage for me?" Papa smiled and nodded and gave her a cabbage with a kiss. Then Harlequin demanded, "Can I have some lettuce?" Papa nodded and gave Harlequin lettuce. Next, Lilac demanded eggplant and Papa gave her eggplant. And little Rex got his radish too. Then Papa Bunny gave Mama Bunny a basket of vegetables. The bunny family happily chomped vegetables. Papa and Mama Bunny looked on contentedly at the little bunnies. Mama said, "Thank God, we have a vegetable garden!"

15 The Ox Who Envied the Pig

Big Red and Little Red were two brother oxen who worked on a farm. The farmer's wife ordered that a pig should be fattened for their daughter's wedding. Little Red envied the pig when he saw the good food the pig got to eat. He complained to Big Red, "We get only grass and straw whereas the pig eats much better food." "The pig is being given good food only to be killed," consoled Big Red. But the young ox was still sad. A few days later, the pig was killed and cooked for the wedding feast. Big Red said to his brother, "Now you see what has happened to the pig? The food he ate was just to fatten him for this day." Little Red then realised that it was better to eat simple food and live longer than eat delicious food for only a few days.

16   The Bag of Salt

The lion, the hyena, the tiger, the zebra, the ostrich and the snake met at the waterhole. Just then, the lion spotted a bag on the ground. He sniffed at it and cried, "It's salt!" They were very excited. The zebra said, "Let's eat it." So, the ostrich pecked a hole in it and the salt trickled out. All the animals took turns in tasting it. Very soon, they began to fight over who should keep the salt. A clever jackal was passing by. He told them, "Close your eyes and count to hundred. Whoever finds it first, can keep it," he said. When the animals opened their eyes they found both the jackal and the bag gone!

17   Rabbit the Hunter

One day, Hunter Rabbit went hunting. Suddenly, he saw a track of big footprints and thought they belonged to a giant. He found nothing to hunt in the forest and thought that the giant must have hunted everything. Hunter Rabbit returned home empty-handed and ate berries for dinner. The next day, Hunter Rabbit left early but found nothing. He was tired of eating berries. "I must do something," he declared. This time, he decided to lay a net. But the next day Hunter Rabbit found that a hole had been made in the net. Now, Hunter Rabbit's grandmother was a magician. "I'll make you a magic net that cannot be cut," she said. Next morning, when Hunter Rabbit went to see his net, he saw a blinding light coming from it. Alas! He had captured the Sun! The Sun said, "Let me out, or else, the world will remain dark forever!" Hunter Rabbit quickly freed the Sun. The Sun kicked Hunter Rabbit on his shoulders in anger and the heat turned them brown. That's why rabbits have brown shoulders and still eat berries.

18 A Bad Dream

Roderick was a small cat that lived in Mr. Geddes's house. Every day, he would go to the kitchen to raid his stock of fish, milk and cheese.

One day, he had so much food that his tummy was uncomfortably full. That night he slept on his side. He tossed and turned all night and dreamt of Tiger, Mr. Geddes's dog, chasing him all over the place. Roderick woke up with a pounding heart. Next day, he was still greedy for more and went to the kitchen and ate a lot again. That night too he had bad dreams. The following day when he went to the kitchen, he found Tiger guarding the food. So he could not have his milk and fish. "Ok!" he thought, "I will have black berries and hazelnuts today." That night he didn't have any bad dreams. He decided that he would never eat too much again.

19 The Talking Mule

There once lived a farmer who owned a mule. He made the mule work hard the whole week but on Sunday he allowed it to rest. One Sunday, the farmer had to attend a funeral and so he told his son to saddle the mule. When the son approached the mule, the mule said, "Why are you making me work on a Sunday?" The farmer's son ran away in fright and told his father about the talking mule. The farmer too was frightened out of his wits on hearing the mule talk. The farmer's wife and the dog were also terrified. "I don't believe this! It's the strangest thing that has ever happened," exclaimed the farmer's wife. The cat which was sitting nearby listening to them, purred, "What is so strange? Haven't you heard that a talking mule has entered the country?" Hearing the cat talk too, the farmer's wife fainted!

20 Mac the Mouse

Tom the cat always chased Mac the mouse. One day, when Mac sneaked into the kitchen, Tom set chase again. Mac ran for his life and hid inside the library. While Tom watched the entrance of the library, Mac found a pile of interesting books. He read them and gained knowledge on how to outsmart a cat. However, after a while he was hungry. Peeking around, he noticed Tom—fast asleep. Mac tiptoed across and was about to enter the kitchen, when he heard a loud, "Meow!" He jumped out of the kitchen and ran inside his hole. As Tom guarded the hole all day, Mac thought, "I might not have learnt how to outwit a cat as yet, but I have learnt enough to save myself."

21 The Fox and the Grapes

One hot summer day, a fox was looking for food. He roamed about for a long time but could get nothing. His stomach growled in hunger and his throat was dry with thirst. He was cursing his luck when he found himself inside a farm-yard. He saw a bunch of ripe, juicy grapes on a vine hanging high on a branch. His mouth watered at the sight. Moving back a few paces, he jumped high to get hold of the grapes. But the grapes were too high for him to reach. He tried again and again but failed each time. Finally he grew tired and walked away saying, "I'm sure these grapes are sour. So I don't want them anymore."

A crow sitting on a tree, nearby laughed at the fox for showing disinterest because he was unable to get what he wanted.

22 The King's White Elephant

There lived some carpenters on the bank of a river. One day, an elephant came limping to their huts. The carpenters took out the big splinter from the elephant's foot and took care of him until he recovered. The grateful elephant helped the carpenters by pulling trees and rolling the logs to the river. The carpenters looked after him and fed him well. The elephant had a son who was strong and beautiful and white in colour. When the elephant grew old, he said to his son, "You must help the carpenters as they helped me once when I was in great need."

One day, the king saw the beautiful white elephant and wanted to own him. He paid the carpenters a good price for the elephant and took him home. The king took good care of the elephant as long as he lived.

23 Mrs. Cottontail and Her Family

Mrs. Cottontail loved all animals. She lived in a boot-shaped house with lots of animals. Cats, dogs, mice, rabbits, bears and birds—all lived happily together. Mrs. Cottontail cooked for them, bathed them and played with them. All her family loved her. One day the phone rang. "You must come to help me!" sobbed someone. It was her aunt who had broken her leg. Mrs. Cottontail hastily made arrangements to go. She requested her neighbour, Mrs. Hare, "Please look after my family." Mrs. Hare didn't like animals. Once Mrs. Cottontail left, she put up her feet. "Don't disturb me while I enjoy my cup of tea," she said. Soon a fight broke out over a piece of carrot between two rabbits. Mrs. Hare grabbed the carrot and ate it up. When Margie the bear pushed another bear, she locked her inside a room. The animals were very sad. When Mrs. Cottontail returned, all the animals rushed to her. She hugged them and promised never to leave them again.

24 How the Swan Got a Long Neck

There was once a large lake which was shared by ducks and swans. The shape of the lake resembled that of a swan and so was named the Swan Lake. After this, the proud swans did not allow the ducks to swim along with them. This made the ducks angry. One day, while the ducks and swans were quarrelling about who would swim in the lake, a flock of geese were passing by. The geese listened to both sides and said, "The swans should be allowed to swim first because they are prettier than ducks." But one old wise goose declared, "Let us all share the lake since it is large enough." The swans did not like this idea and a fight broke out among all the birds. The geese bit and pulled the swans' necks and as a result, their necks became longer. That's why swans have long necks even today.

25 Boris' New Friends

Boris was a grumpy bear who did not have any friends. He growled at the other animals because he thought that no one liked him. One day, he was tired after a long walk and fell asleep on the top of a hill. Some animals passing by saw his fluffy body and crowded around him, cuddling him. When Boris awoke, he saw many animals playfully tickling him. They were the mouse, the beaver, the rabbit, the sloth and the birds. Seeing them around him, at first he was angry and was about to drive them away. Then he realised how lonely he was and how much he needed friends. He joined them in their play. From that day, Boris went up the hill every day and his new friends would come there and play with him. He was no longer lonely or grumpy. Now he became a cheerful bear.

26 The Tortoise and the Geese

There lived a tortoise in a tank who had two geese as his friends. They would spend time together and play in the tank. The days passed happily. One day there was a drought in the region and all the rivers and tanks dried up. This was followed by a famine and there was nothing to eat. Animals were dying and birds were flying to new places. The geese also decided to fly away to some other place.

When they went to the tortoise to bid him farewell, he said, "Please take me along. I'll die if I live here." "But you cannot fly like us, so how can we take you?" the geese asked.

The tortoise had a plan. The geese would hold the two ends of a stick with their beaks while flying and he would hold the middle of the stick with his teeth. The geese agreed to the tortoise's suggestion but they warned him not to say a word while they were flying, otherwise, he would fall down. The geese flew over rivers and hills and forests while the tortoise tightly held the stick with his teeth. People who saw the unusual sight cried out in wonder, "Oh! What a strange sight! Have you ever seen two birds carrying a tortoise like that?" The tortoise did not like that and said, "What is amusing those fools?" No sooner did he utter those words, than his mouth lost its grip on the stick and he fell down to the ground and died.

27 The Spider, Hare and the Moon

The Moon had watched the people on Earth for many years and saw that they all were afraid of death. She said to the Spider, "Go to Earth and tell the people there that there is nothing to be afraid of death." So, the Spider started moving towards the Earth through moonbeams and sunbeams. On the way, he met a Hare. The Spider asked the Hare to carry the Moon's message to the Earth. The Hare, as usual, was in a hurry. He didn't even hear the complete message. "All the people on the Earth will die!" he proclaimed on reaching Earth. When the Moon heard this, she angrily hit him on the nose for giving the wrong message. That's why the Hare still has a split lip. Then she asked the Spider to go back to the Earth to give the correct message. The Spider is still giving the message, spinning and weaving quietly.

28 The Cat and Venus

Once a cat saw a handsome young man and fell in love with him. She begged Venus the goddess, "Please, Venus, change me into a woman. I love this young man and wish to marry him." Venus heard her request and seeing her earnestness, changed the cat into a beautiful young maiden. The young man saw the maiden and fell in love with her beauty. He decided to make her his wife. The two were very happy. One day, Venus thought, "Let me test if the cat still retains her animal habits even after getting a human form." She sent a mouse to run past the chamber. Seeing the scampering mouse, the cat, who was now a maiden, forgot everything and chased the mouse. Venus was disappointed by her behaviour and turned her back into a cat.

29 The Foolish, Timid Rabbit

"Thud! Bump!" The foolish rabbit sleeping under a tree, jumped in fright and ran for his life. "The earth is breaking! Help!" he cried. On the way, another rabbit asked him why he was running. "Run! The earth is breaking!" panted the rabbit. On hearing this, the second rabbit started to run behind the first rabbit. Next, the deer, the fox and the elephant followed.

The lion saw them running and asked. "Why are you running?" The rabbit told him that he had heard the sound of the earth breaking up. The lion said, "Take me to the place where you heard that sound." There, the lion examined the place for a while and roared, "You foolish rabbit, it was the sound of a coconut falling on the ground that you heard!" The other animals felt ashamed of their foolishness and crept away in shame.

30 The Fox and the Geese

One day, a fox came to a meadow where he saw some fine, fat geese. He thought that they would make a good meal for him. When the geese realised that the fox was planning to eat them, they begged for mercy and cried in fear. But the fox had no pity for them. Finally, one goose courageously said, "Before we die, please allow us to say our prayers so that God forgives our sins. Then you can choose the fattest goose amongst us."

The fox thought it was a reasonable request and agreed to it. Then the first goose began her prayer. She kept repeating "Ga! Ga!" continuously. Soon the second goose followed her and then the third. Finally the fox grew tired of waiting and walked away sulking in anger. The moment the fox was out of sight, the clever geese stopped their prayers and hastily left the place.

31 How the Zebra Got Its Stripes

Long ago, zebras were spotless white. They looked somewhat like a horse and somewhat like a donkey. They were very beautiful. They lived in the forest faraway from mankind. Very few people really knew what a zebra looked like.

Zuzu was a young zebra and like all young ones, he was very naughty! He was also very adventurous. "Don't wander alone," his mother often warned. And little Zuzu always answered, "Yes, Mama."

But one day, Zuzu was bored. Everyone was busy in their work. He had nobody to play with. So he decided to roam the forest by himself. "I'll be back in some time. Mama wouldn't even know that I was gone," he thought. He wandered about in the forest and forgot the time. After a while, when he looked around, he didn't know where he was. He was lost!

"What is this place?" he exclaimed in astonishment. He had reached a village! Soon he was surrounded by strange creatures. They were actually the people of that village but Zuzu had never seen humans before. He was terrified. "Look! What a beautiful animal," said someone. "Let's catch him and keep him with us," said another. Zuzu was petrified. He missed his mother and was sorry for not paying attention to her warnings. "Oh! I wish I had paid heed to Mama's warning," he wailed. Frightened, he ran to escape from the people. He looked for a place to hide.

Soon, he found a drum of black paint and jumped in. When he emerged, he saw the paint had spread over his body in the form of black wavy lines. When the villagers found him, they thought he had lost his beauty, so they decided to let him go.

Zuzu ran till he reached home. All the zebras were glad to see him. Zuzu explained how he had got black and white stripes all over his body.

The zebras decided to do the same thing so that people would keep away from them. After sometime, all the zebras were born that way, but God made them look beautiful with their black and white stripes.

Contents

The Story of the Month

The Frog Who Became an Emperor

01 The Frog Who Became an Emperor

A woman was to give birth to a baby. Her husband had to leave home in search of a livelihood. Before leaving, he gave his wife a few pieces of silver saying, "Bring up the child with care." Days passed and the woman gave birth to a frog child. She was heartbroken but decided to bring up the frog child with love. One day the frog child said, "Father is coming back tonight. I'm going to meet him on the way."

The man was sad to know that the frog was his child but he found it extraordinary that the frog had known that he was returning home that night. "How did you know that I was returning today?" he asked. The frog replied, "I know everything that is going to happen in this world." Then the frog told his parents that their country was in great danger. "Father, please take me to the emperor. I will defeat the enemy and save my country," he pleaded.

At the emperor's palace, they saw a decree that said that the emperor would marry his daughter to the person who defeated the enemy. The frog told the emperor that he would fight the enemy and defeat them. "How will you fight them?" asked the emperor. "All I need are some hot, glowing embers," said the frog. The emperor arranged for the embers to be brought. The frog sat in front of the fire for three days, devouring the heat. As the invaders entered the city, the frog who was sitting atop the city gate, spat fire, creating panic and confusion amongst them. The enemy fled in terror. The emperor was overjoyed. As a reward, he made the frog a general but said nothing of the princess. After some time the emperor declared that the princess would marry the man who could catch a ball which would be thrown in the air by the emperor's men. Many princes tried their luck and failed. The frog disguised himself as a young man and went to try his luck. He was the only suitor

who managed to catch it. The emperor married his daughter to the young man. Soon the princess realised that her husband would be a frog by day and change into a man at night. She told her father about this. The emperor was taken aback and asked the royal magician. The magician told the emperor that the frog skin was enchanted and could make the wearer live for thousands of years. The greedy emperor asked the young man to let him try the skin. Lo! As soon as he did, the emperor became a frog and the young man became the emperor.

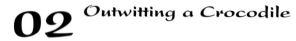

02   *Outwitting a Crocodile*

Sang Kancil was a cunning and witty mouse deer. A number of times, he had managed to trick Sang Buaya, the big, bad crocodile who was always waiting for a chance to eat him. One day, he saw some ripe, juicy fruit on the other side of the river. He wondered how to cross the river without being caught by Sang Buaya and the other crocodiles. He thought for some time and then struck upon a clever idea. He called out to Sang Buaya and told him that the king was having a feast for all animals. He wanted to know how many crocodiles were there. Excited to hear about the party, all the crocodiles lined up across the river to be counted. Crafty Sang Kancil stepped on each of the crocodiles to count them and crossed the river. Once he reached the bank, he laughed heartily at the foolish crocodiles.

03   *The Ass and His Masters*

An ass, who worked for a herbseller, was very sad because his master made him work a lot but gave him very little food. "O God, please get me another master," he prayed daily. God warned the ass that he would regret this decision. However, the ass was stubborn and so God granted him his wish. Soon, the ass was sold to a tile maker but the new master was even worse because he made the ass work even harder. Once more, the ass prayed to God for a change of master. God said, "This is the last time I'm granting your request." Soon the ass's master became disgusted with him for not wanting to work and sold him to a tanner. The ass realised that now his situation was even worse than before. He now regretted always being dissatisfied with his lot and not trying to be happy.

04 The Goatherd and the Wild Goats

A goatherd took his goats to graze every day. One evening, on his way home, some wild goats entered the flock. The goatherd brought them home along with his own. The next day, it snowed heavily and the goatherd could not take the goats out. He gave his own goats just enough to eat but fed the other goats well in the hope of making them stay longer. When the snow thawed, the goatherd took the goats out to graze. At once, the wild goats scampered away to the forest. "You ungrateful creatures!" the goatherd shouted, "I cared for you more than my own goats and now you are leaving me!" The wild goats replied that they did not trust him since he had neglected his old goats for new ones. He might do the same to them one day.

05 The Great Big Dog

Willie and John were returning from school when they saw a big dog. He was limping. John said, "I think he has hurt himself. We should help him." Willie held out his hand for the dog to sniff. "You should always let a dog sniff you before touching him," he said. "Look! He's wagging his tail. We are friends now." They pulled out the thorn that was stuck in his paw. "Wuff!" thanked the dog and went away.

A few days later, the boys were crossing the road when a car came speeding around the corner. Suddenly a brown shape flashed across the road and pushed John out of the way. It was the dog they had helped! "Here, Buster," they heard a voice call and the dog's owner, a boy of their own age, came running up. "He saved my life," said John giving the dog a hug. "I think he's glad that he got the chance to repay your good deed," said the boy. Buster wagged his tail vigorously.

06 The Foolish Monkey

A monkey fell in love with a beautiful young girl. He dressed up as a man and went to her house. Mr. Monkey was so impressed by the welcome he received that the next time he took his friend to the girl's house. The girl's father asked the friend questions about his daughter's suitor. Seeing the monkey's good fortune, his friend was jealous.

He replied, "My friend is good as well as rich. But there's a secret he has which I'll tell you later."

Mr. Monkey invited his friend on his wedding day. After dinner, his friend began to sing and listening to him all the monkeys started dancing. Soon, Mr. Monkey also joined them! He jumped so wildly that his tail came out of his clothes and everyone saw that he was a monkey. The girl's father gave Mr. Monkey a good hiding and chased him away.

07 The Bird and the Bat

Once, a bird would sing sweetly all night when all her other companions were asleep. One day, a bat asked the bird why she sang only at night. The bird replied, "Once when I was singing during the day, a fowler heard me singing and followed me till he trapped me in his net. I managed to escape and since then I sing only at night when no human being will be able to hear me." The bat said, "But it's no use doing that now because you are free now. If you had been more careful when you were free, then you would not have been captured in the first place. One should be careful at the right time." "You are right," replied the bird and decided to take the bat's advice. She started singing during the day as well and put her past behind.

08 The Cross Caterpillar

There once lived a grumpy green and yellow cater-pillar in a cabbage. If other caterpillars would come too close to him, he would frown and glare at them. One day a white butterfly with black spots sat down on the same leaf and decided to lay her eggs there. "You can't lay your eggs here," said the caterpillar. The butterfly just laughed and laid neat rows of eggs and flew away. The caterpillar grumbled and said he would get rid of them. But soon he started feeling sleepy. He made a little silken hammock and went to sleep. Three weeks later, he awoke and chewed his way out of his cocoon. To his amazement he had become a butterfly—with white wings that had black spots on it! He was sorry that he had acted so foolishly over the eggs.

09 The Lost Possum

Mr. Possum lived with his wife and three children—Polly, Paula and Percy in a tall tree. They were a happy family. Mr. and Mrs. Possum slept on the higher branches while the children slept on the lower branches and like all possums, they would hang by their tails while they slept.

One morning, Mr. and Mrs. Possum woke up to find Percy missing. They called the other children and asked them if they had seen Percy. "No, Mama," said Paula and Polly. He was nowhere to be seen. He wasn't in the woods and he wasn't down by the lake. At last, Mrs. Possum spotted him near a beehive hanging from a tree. He was busy scoop-ing honey into his mouth. Mr. Possum shouted, "Percy, come down at once!" Percy left the beehive, licking his sticky paws. "You are a very naughty pos-sum," scolded his mother. She took him down to the lake and washed his fur. "I am feeling cold," whined Percy. He decided that he was not going to sneak off again to the beehive. But from that day on, Percy slept with his parents in the upper branches so that they could keep an eye on him.

10 The Cat and the Mice

Once, there was a house that was full of mice. A cat decided to move into the house. She caught the mice one by one and ate them up. The mice were very frightened and decided to remain in their holes. Now the cat found it difficult to catch more mice, so she thought of a trick to fool them. She climbed up the wall and let herself hang down by her hind legs to appear as if she were dead. She thought that she would be able to trap the mice in this way. After a little while, a mouse peeped out of his hole and saw the cat. He understood that the cat was trying to trick them. The mouse said, "Madam Cat, even if you turn yourself into food, we will not come near you!" The cat soon left the house and the mice were happy again.

11 The Musical Donkey

A washerman had a lean and thin donkey. He would carry heavy loads of clothes in the daytime but at night he was free. One day, the donkey met a jackal and they became friends. One night, they entered a garden full of ripe cucumbers and ate to their heart's content. After that, they went to the garden every night to eat cucumbers. One night while eating cucumbers, the donkey said to the jackal, "It is such a lovely night. I feel like singing a song." The jackal replied, "Uncle, if you sing, the farmers will hear you and drive us away. Besides, your voice is not so pleasant." But the donkey told the jackal that he had no taste for music and started braying. The farmers heard him and came out of their houses with sticks. They beat the donkey and drove him away. They even tied a heavy mortar round his neck. The jackal was watching the scene from outside and felt sorry for his friend. When the farmers had gone he told the stupid donkey, "Congratulations, Uncle! I told you that the farmers would give you a fitting reward if they hear you." The donkey was sorry for not listening to the jackal.

12 Bambi

Deep in a beautiful green forest, a baby deer was born. His mother decided to call him Bambi. All the animals came to see the little fawn. Bambi was golden brown in colour with thin spindly legs. A little rabbit called Thumper was very curious about the new arrival. "Can I be your friend?" he asked Bambi, thumping his feet in excitement. "Yes," replied Bambi. Thumper and Bambi became friends from that day onwards. They wandered in the forest and made new friends. One day while they were in the meadow they heard a loud bang! "What's that?" asked Bambi startled, his nose twitching nervously. "That's a hunter," said Thumper. "My mother always says you have to be really careful of them." "So did mine," said Bambi and they ran all the way home to safety.

13 A Bunny's Tail

Bup the bunny was very vain but he didn't like his bobtail. He wished to have a long tail. One day, he came across a long tail in the woods. It belonged to a toy cat that a little boy had been playing with. Bup took it and ran back to his burrow to attach it to himself. When the other rabbits asked him what he was doing inside, he said proudly, "I am growing a tail." On the seventh day he came out and showed off his new tail. All the other rabbits wanted to grow one as well. "Please tell us how to grow one," they begged. "You have to stay in your burrows and think about tails for seven days," said Bup. The silly rabbits believed him and tried their best—but of course, they couldn't grow their tails! Bup told them that since he was the cleverest, he should be their king. They had a meeting on Breezy Hill to talk about it. Suddenly, a fox sneaked up on them. All the rabbits fled but poor Bup was slowed down by his long tail. The fox grabbed the tail and it came off in his mouth. The other rabbits realised that Bup had been pretending. Poor Bup felt ashamed and hid in his burrow.

14   Brer Rabbit and the Little Girl

Brer Rabbit was very fond of lettuce. One day, he came across many rows of lettuce in a field. A wire fence surrounded the field. While he stood there thinking how to get in, a little girl entered the field through a gate. She picked some lettuce and left. Brer Rabbit quickly thought of a plan. The next day, when the little girl came, he said, "Hello, how's your father, Mr. Farmer, today? He told me that I can visit the field whenever I want." The girl believed Brer Rabbit and let him in. Brer Rabbit ate lettuce to his heart's content. The next morning, he went to the field again. On the third day, when the farmer saw three rows of lettuce missing, he questioned his daughter. She told him about Brer Rabbit. The farmer realised what the wily rabbit was up to. The next day, when Brer Rabbit arrived, the farmer was waiting for him. He tied him tightly and left him in the field. Brer Rabbit pleaded but in vain. At last the kind girl took pity and untied him. Brer Rabbit fled. But he didn't forget to pluck a few more lettuce on his way out!

15   The Hare and the Merchant

A hare invited his friends, the thrush, the oriole and the crow to his home. The hare suggested that they play a prank on two greedy merchants who had come to the grasslands to make money and were busy counting their money on an abacus. One merchant was quite bald. The crow perched on his head. The merchant cursed the crow and told the other merchant to drive it away. A moment later, the crow perched on the bald man's head again. The other merchant picked up the abacus to hit the crow, but it flew away and the abacus hit the bald man's head. The birds and the hare roared with laughter. They made such a noise, chirping and cackling that the merchants could not continue with their work. They picked their bags and left the place.

16 The Peacock and the Tortoise

A tortoise who lived in a stream was good friend of a peacock who lived in a tree near by. One day, a bird catcher trapped the peacock. The bird begged him to let him say goodbye to his friend, the tortoise. The tortoise asked the bird catcher if he would let the peacock go if he was given a gift. The man agreed and the tortoise dived into the stream and emerged with a pearl. The man was satisfied with the gift and set the peacock free. Very soon his greed got the better of him and he returned to the stream. He demanded that the tortoise bring him another pearl or else he would capture the peacock Angry with the man's greedy ways, the tortoise told the man to give him the pearl so that he could find its identical twin in the stream. But of course, he didn't! He swam away and left the foolish man empty-handed.

17 Bunny Rabbit Falls in Love

Bunny Rabbit was in love and could think of nothing else but his ladylove. When Miss Meadows asked him what the matter was, he told her that he was in love with one of her girls but didn't have the courage to speak to her. Miss Meadows chided him for being a coward. Soon, he saw his ladylove coming along. Bunny Rabbit summoned all his courage and went up to her and asked, "You are so lovely. Why aren't you married? The girl replied, "I've been looking for the right sign." Bunny Rabbit said, "If you'd told me about it, you would have found your husband." "And who would that be?" asked the girl. "Me, of course," said Bunny Rabbit. On hearing this, the girl walked away in a huff. Bunny Rabbit now started thinking of ways in which he could show the right sign to her. He sang loudly:

"This little girl is looking for a sign,
She'll see her lover down by the big pine."

Next morning, the girl walked to the pine tree. Bunny Rabbit was waiting for her. The girl realised that Bunny Rabbit was fooling her and went away. Poor Bunny Rabbit was left all alone.

18 Stones for a Horse

Tom was a lazy little boy who lived in a farm. One day, his father asked him to take Bess the horse to another farm where she was needed for the day. "Oh, Dad," grumbled Tom, "It's Saturday. I want to go play." "You can play after you get back," replied his father sternly. So Tom set off with Bess who was a big, brown, gentle horse. "Hurry up!" shouted Tom as Bess struggled to climb the steep slope leading to the farm. Then he lost his temper and started throwing pebbles at her to make her go faster. "Hey! Stop that," shouted his friend, Billy who had come looking for him. Billy picked up a handful of pebbles and scattered them under Bess's feet. To Tom's surprise, Bess was able to trot faster since she could get a better grip on the road. Tom patted Bess in apology.

19 Let's See on Which Side the Camel Sits

A grocer and a potter decided to share a camel to carry their goods to the market. Each one filled a pannier with his goods and placed it on the camel. As they walked along the road, the hungry camel would take a bite out of the pannier containing the grocer's green vegetables. The potter noticed what the camel was doing and chuckled to himself, "As long as my pots are fine, why should I care what he does with the vegetables?" He felt he had the best of the bargain and did not bother to tell his companion what was going on.

When they reached the market, the camel had to sit down. He sat down on the heavier side, crushing the potter's wares under him. The potter was horrified. Now he wished he had stopped the camel. In wishing to harm someone else he had harmed himself as well.

20 The Surprise Basket

Anna was going to her friend's birthday party. "Meow!" she heard a sound and saw Tinker, Mrs. Brown's cat with a kitten in her mouth. Anna, who loved animals, followed her to a barn and saw that Tinker had hidden her three kittens there. "I should take them into the house," thought Anna to herself though she knew she was going to spoil her dress. She put the kittens in a box and carried them to Mrs. Brown who thanked her gladly. Tinker looked at the box in dismay. "I have been looking for them everywhere," exclaimed the old lady. By then, it was too late to go to the party. Sadly Anna returned home and told her mother what had happened. The next morning, Anna's mother handed her a basket with a smile. Anna peeped in and shouted with joy. Mrs. Brown had sent her a kitten!

21 Brave Tomasso

Once there lived a pair of beautiful cats called Tomasso and Lilia. Their fur were as white as snow and as soft as silk. They always kept themselves very clean. The other animals thought them to be very proud, as they did not mix with other cats. The other cats were very jealous of them. One cat said, "I am sure Tomasso is a coward." Another cat added, "I agree." One day, when Tomasso and Lilia were walking down the street, a huge dog blocked their way and growled ferociously. The cats were frightened. The dog tried to jump on Lilia but Tomasso attacked the dog. The dog was completely taken aback and fled. Even the people on the street were amazed to see a dog being overcome by a cat. The news of Tomasso's bravery spread throughout the region. But Tomasso was not affected by the praise showered on him. Lilia was very proud of the scratch that Tomasso had got while fighting the dog. "This scar will be a reminder of Tomasso's courage," she declared. After that incident, the other cats became friends with Tomasso and Lilia.

22 The Parrot

A grocer kept a parrot in a cage that hung outside his shop. One day, the parrot saw the grocer mixing sand in the sugar. When a customer entered the shop to buy sugar, the parrot cried loudly, "Sand in the sugar." Hearing this, the woman left the shop at once. "I will wring your neck if you don't keep quiet," threatened the grocer. But the next day, when a customer came to buy cocoa, the parrot shouted, "The cocoa contains brick dust!" The grocer advanced to catch the bird but the parrot begged, "Spare me for the last time. I promise never to open my mouth again." But when a woman came to buy butter, the parrot screeched, "There's lard in the butter!" The grocer threw the parrot into the ash pit but the parrot survived and flew away in search of a land where truth was respected.

23 Fred and the Lily Pad

Fred the frog lived on a mushroom and was looking for a new home. One day he hopped onto the back of a passing turtle. He admired a squirrel's tree house as he passed by. "It must have a nice view. But it would get tiring climbing up there everyday," he thought. Just then, he saw a worm popping out of its hole. "That's a cozy home but I don't think I would fit in it," said Fred to himself. Then he saw a rabbit running into its burrow. He knew that rabbits' burrows were connected by tunnels. "I wouldn't like to live with so many room-mates," said Fred to himself. They reached a pond and the turtle slid into the water. All around him Fred saw lily pads of various sizes and insects, which would make a delicious snack. "This will be my new home," he said happily and hopped onto a lily pad.

24 The Fish That Were Too Clever

Two fish and a frog lived in a pond. They were friends. One fish was named Satabuddhi—having the understanding of a hundred, while the other fish was named Sahasrabuddhi—having the understanding of a thousand. The frog was called Ekbuddhi—having the understanding of one. One day, they overheard some fishermen making a plan to catch some fish.

The three of them were frightened and wondered what to do. Sahasrabuddhi said that he knew many ways of escaping and did not fear anyone. Satabuddhi agreed with him but the frog went away with his wife to another pond. The next day, the fisherman trapped Satabuddhi and Sahasrabuddhi in their nets. The frog looked at them from far and said to his wife, "I, who have the understanding of only one, am safe while those with the understanding of a hundred and thousand are trapped."

25 Why the Bat Has No Friends

Once, there was a battle between the birds and the animals. A bat was wondering whose side he should take. He went to the birds and said that he was with them because he had wings. But the animals defeated the birds. After the battle, the bat joined the animals who were celebrating their victory. The animals asked, "What are you doing here?" The bat replied, "How can I be a bird? I have teeth." The next day there was another battle. This time the birds attacked the animals with their beaks and defeated them. Now the cunning bat joined the birds and said, "I have wings, so I am a bird." Each time the bat would join the winning side. Finally, the birds and animals decided to live in peace. When the chiefs of both sides came to know what the bat had done, they punished him. He was told that now he could fly only at night. That is why bats are friendless and awake only when the rest of the animal kingdom is asleep.

26 The Foolish Camel

One day, the beasts of the jungle decided to have a party. The lion who was the king of the jungle, sent out invitations to all the animals, big and small. There was a lot of merrymaking and noise. This was followed by a grand feast. Happy, the monkey performed a dance. He jumped and swayed gracefully. Everyone clapped loudly at the end of his performance. The monkey couldn't stop smiling. However, the camel who was present was jealous of the praise showered on the monkey. He too wished for the same attention from the others. He stood up and started to dance. Everyone laughed at his ungainly and awkward movements. Soon the other animals drove the poor camel out. The camel felt hurt. He realised too late that he had made a fool of himself by trying to ape the monkey just to be appreciated by others.

27 The Lark and Her Young Ones

A lark once built her nest on a wheat plant. One day, the farmer came to see the crops. He looked around and said, "I think it's time to harvest the crop now. I'll ask my neighbours to help me." One young lark overheard this and was frightened. He told his mother about the farmer's words. "Mamma, let's move to a safer place." The mother said, "Don't worry, Son. I don't think it is necessary to move out right now. When a person calls his friends for help, it means that the situation is not urgent." A few days later, the farmer once again visited the field and saw that the wheat was fully ripe. He said to himself, "Tomorrow I will come to harvest the wheat myself." When the lark heard these words, she knew the time had come when she must move her family to a new place immediately.

28 The Ass Carrying the Image

One day, an ass was carrying an image of a deity to be placed in the temple. Seeing the glorious image of the idol, people bowed down reverentially. The ass thought that they were paying their respects to him. He puffed up with pride and importance. With his head held high, he stopped and nodded every time someone bowed before the deity. His master waited for him to go forward and tugged at his reign many times. But the foolish ass did not pay heed to his master's directions. Suddenly he felt something hard on his back. He screamed in pain, "Ouch!!" It was his master's whip which had lashed against his body. His master said, "Oh, you fool! You thought people would worship an ass? How silly of you to take credit for something that belongs to someone else! Get on your way!"

The ass bent his head in shame and carried on his way.

Contents

The Story of the Month

A Little Help from a Friend

01 A Little Help from a Friend

Martin a small grey mouse and Rusty a big bull, lived in a valley. Rusty would often step on Martin and the latter would cry out in pain, "Why don't you look where you are going? You'll kill me one day!" "I have better things to do than look down with every step I take. You should be more careful," the bull would say. Things did not improve with time.

Finally, tired of fighting, they decided to have a contest. "This place is not big enough for both of us," declared Rusty. "Whoever swims across to the other side of the lake first, will have the right to live here," Martin readily agreed.

So one day, the race began. Both of them stood at the edge of the lake on the assigned day. Rusty let Martin begin first. Then Rusty jumped into the water. He created such a big splash that Martin was thrown back on the shore. Rusty laughed uproariously

while swimming away at a rapid pace. Martin sat miserably on the shore. Suddenly a big, green head appeared out of the water. "Hi! I'm Nessy the dinosaur. I live in this lake. Why are you so sad?" Martin related his sad story—how he would lose the race and soon have to leave his home.

Nessy was a kindhearted dinosaur. He felt sorry for Martin and offered to help him. He said to Martin, "Climb on my back and I'll carry you across to the other side. You will reach faster than the bull. But I'll keep my body under the water so that Rusty does not see me. As soon as we reach the shore, I will sink in the water and you can swim the remaining distance yourself." "Thank you for being so kind," said Martin gratefully.

Martin jumped on Nessy's back and off they went! Very soon Martin could see Rusty a little ahead of him. Rusty wondered how Martin had caught up with him so soon. Nessy remained hidden underwater and as soon as they neared the shore Martin jumped off and swam the rest of the distance. When Rusty reached the shore and saw Martin already there, he bellowed with rage. He could not believe that a small mouse had defeated him. He stomped off into the jungle in anger. A little later, Nessy reappeared to take Martin back to the valley.

When they reached the valley, Martin hopped off and thanked Nessy for his help. Nessy said, "Let me know if anyone bothers you and I'll be there at once." Martin was delighted to be back home, alone and safe. He could see Rusty standing on the hillside across the lake. From that day on, Martin and Nessy were fast friends and could often be seen playing together.

02 All Work and No Play

It was a hot and lazy summer day. "Wake up, lazybones. Time to finish your work!" said Mrs. Hippo to her children. Harry, Hugh, Hallie and Honey groaned. "Mama, it's too hot to work," protested Harry. "But a perfect day to swim in the river and chase butterflies," said Hallie dreamily. Mrs. Hippo said, "You can do that after work."

"Let's swim first and work later," suggested Harry. They had such a good time wallowing in the mud and splashing water that they forgot the time. When Mama arrived, she was very angry. "No pudding after supper for anyone!" she declared as punishment. Now the hippos felt sorry for not listening to her. Next morning, the four hippos left home early to do their work. Mrs. Hippo was happy and gave each of them a bowl of pudding. "It is never good to disobey Mama," said Honey enjoying her pudding.

03 The Flea and the Ox

A flea and an ox used to live in the same stall. The flea used to watch the ox carry tons of loads every day. He felt sorry for the ox. One day, when the ox was about to go to bed after a hard day's work, the flea asked the ox, "Why do you bear the burden of men and slave tirelessly? Look at me. I am a much smaller creature but I do no work. I suck their blood and roam about freely!"

"I am not an ungrateful animal," replied the ox. "I am loved and well cared for. Besides, my master often pats my shoulders and head for the hard work that I do for them," he explained.

"Oh, that sounds very good, but I can't survive like that. You see, one little pat from them will kill me instead," replied the flea and flew away.

04 The Mice and the Weasels

The mice were always beaten by the mighty army of weasels. So, a mice council was called. Everybody agreed that they needed an organised army to overcome their enemy. Since they had no leader, there was no discipline among them. They first selected a general and then his core mice. These mice belonged to royal families and were known for their courage and strength. Once the general and his men were selected, the army was set up and the ensign designed. The brave general and his men wore fancy turbans and shiny medals. Once the war began, the weasel army advanced towards the mice. All the mice, including the generals, ran into their holes. Alas! Their huge turbans got stuck at the entrance and they were stranded outside. Meanwhile, the weasels arrived and ate them up. It is rightly said—a false show of strength can bring more danger.

05 The Dog Show

Billy had a dog called Tinker. He was not a very good-looking dog but Billy loved Tinker and looked after him very well. One day he saw a poster: Dog Show on Sunday. "I will take Tinker to the show," he said excitedly. "He is never going to win a prize," his friends laughed, "he is ugly." But Billy had made up his mind. However, at the show the lady who was in charge told him the same thing. Brokenhearted, Billy sat on the side with Tinker, who licked his face to cheer him up. An old man had been watching them. He said, "There's another competition in which you can enter your dog—The Competition for the Best Kept Dog." Billy did and to his delight, Tinker came first! Billy received the prize money proudly and Tinker got a nice red collar.

06 The River Snake

Once, a woman had to cross a flooded river. She stood there wondering what to do when a snake appeared. "I will help you cross the river but you must give me something in return," he said. "When I have a daughter I will marry her to you," promised the woman. Soon the woman gave birth to a daughter. Years passed by. One day the snake reappeared. "I have come to take my bride," he reminded her of the promise. The woman pleaded, but in vain. Finally, she married her daughter to the snake. When the brothers came to know what had happened, they went to the snake and persuaded him to go with them to a beach. There they pushed him into the sea and brought their sister home.

07 Peesnut and the Bears

Peesnut was the beautiful daughter of a tribal chieftain. One day, she went with her friends to the woods to collect flowers and began to sing happily. "Don't sing so loudly! If the bears wake up, they may attack us!" warned her friends.

"I don't care about those ugly bears," she said. "Oh, don't be so stupid!" they warned her again. Suddenly, they realised that Peesnut was no longer with them. "Peesnut, where are you?" they cried in fear but could not find her. A little distance away, Peesnut was busy plucking flowers. Soon, it became dark. "Can I help you, Peesnut?" someone said. She looked up to see a bear. "How do you know my name?" asked Peesnut, surprised. "Who doesn't know the beautiful daughter of the chief?" replied the bear. "It is dark. Why don't you spend the night with us? We shall be honoured," he told her. Peesnut went with the bear to their village. All the bears looked after Peesnut and gave her food and water. They were very kind. Next morning, one of the bears accompanied Peesnut back to the village. Everybody was very happy and rejoiced.

08   Babe the Blue Ox

It was a very cold day. Paul the farmer was walking through the woods when he saw a blue baby ox shivering. Paul took the ox home and kept him near the fireplace. He named him Babe. Babe helped in hauling large logs but he hated working in the summer as the roads were rough. One winter, Babe fell in love with Bessie, a beautiful calf. Paul bought the calf from the farmer. But unlike Babe, Bessie loved the warm, summer

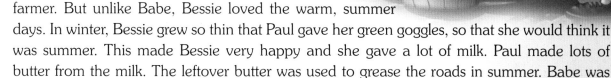

days. In winter, Bessie grew so thin that Paul gave her green goggles, so that she would think it was summer. This made Bessie very happy and she gave a lot of milk. Paul made lots of butter from the milk. The leftover butter was used to grease the roads in summer. Babe was now happy to work even in summers as the roads were smooth.

09   The Wise Monkey and the Foolish Demon

Bruzo lived with his parents in an old banyan tree. He was very mischievous and enjoyed playing pranks all day long. But he was also very wise.

One afternoon while plucking some fruits, Bruzo's mother slipped down from the branch of a fruit tree. "Help! Help!" she shouted. Bruzo's father called the old monkey wizard who knew the remedy for all ailments. "She has fractured her hip bones which can only be cured with the juice of the yellow flowers that grow in the pond guarded by the demon," said the wizard. Bruzo volunteered to go and get the flower for he could not bear to see his mother in pain. The pond was a little distance away from the fruit tree. As Bruzo neared the pond, he could see the huge footprints of the demon in the sand. He carefully waded through the water and as he was about to pluck the flower, the demon popped out of the water and shouted aloud, "How dare you come to my pond? You shall pay with your life and be my meal." Wise Bruzo at once said, "Oh Mighty One, let me eat this flower and dry myself on the land. My meat will taste bitter if you have me wet." The foolish demon believed Bruzo and allowed him to go. Bruzo ran with the flowers and never came back.

10 Elly Learns a Lesson

Elly and Edward were a happy pair of elephants living in the zoo. One day, a giraffe family joined the zoo. Elly rushed to greet the newcomers. She was very impressed by the tall and slender animals. "I wish I could be dainty like them," she told Edward, "I think I will eat less like them." "Don't be silly," scolded Edward.

But the next day, Elly sniffed at the piles of sugarcane that the keepers brought for her. Edward was angry but Elly was unmoved.

That night there was a terrible storm. A huge boulder fell on the giraffe's cage and the poor animals were trapped inside. No one was able to move the boulder. The keepers tied a rope around the boulder and Edward and Elly pulled the rope with all their might. At last the boulder was removed and the giraffes were rescued.

Later Elly said to Edward, "You were right, dear. My strength is useful too."

11 The Fox among the Lion Cubs

A lion found a fox cub while hunting. Feeling sorry for the whimpering creature, the lion took it home. The lioness had recently given birth to cubs and decided to bring up the fox along with her cubs.

The fox and lion cubs grew up together. One day while playing, the cubs saw a ram. The lion cubs wanted to fight it but the fox, true to his nature, was scared. He urged, "Let us run away." When they returned home, the cubs related the incident to their mother. The lioness understood that a fox can never be a lion even if he is brought up among lions. She said to the fox, "I will take you to your own people. You might be in danger if you stay with us." The next day, the lion family said goodbye to the fox. The lioness took the cub and left him near a pack of fox.

12 Mrs. Rabbit's Sale

"We need another room!" declared Mrs. Rabbit. "Yes, dear. But where is the money?" said Mr. Rabbit. "Let's have a garden sale! My friends will help," said Rabbit Junior.

All week long, the other animals brought things they didn't need to Mrs. Rabbit's house. On the day of the sale, the garden was crowded with eager buyers. Before long, most of the things were sold.

"Where are my glasses?" said Mr. Rabbit later. Mrs. Rabbit and her bunnies were silent. The glasses had been sold off by mistake!

They were wondering what to do when there was a knock on the door. It was Mrs. Hen. She said "I bought these glasses thinking that they would be fine for me. But I can't see through them. Perhaps you can sell them to someone they'll be useful for." Mrs. Rabbit immediately recognised the glasses. "Yes, I indeed know someone who'll need them," said Mrs. Rabbit with a twinkle in her eye.

13 The Heron and the Hummingbird

The heron and the hummingbird both loved to eat fish. One day, the hummingbird said to the heron, "There doesn't seem to be enough fish for both of us. The first person to perch atop the tree by the river will get all the fish."

Both the birds started their flight from the same spot. The heron flew steadily without stopping while the hummingbird would keep stopping at flowers along the way to suck nectar. Sometimes he would sleep. When the hummingbird saw that the heron was far ahead, he zipped past and overtook the heron. But again he would stop by some flower along the way. Finally, the heron reached the tree-top and so became the owner of all the fish. "I think I like the nectar from the flowers better!" said the hummingbird. The hummingbird, since then, only sucks nectar from the flowers while the heron catches fish from the river.

14   Give the Cat a Bone

Suzy was a playful cat who loved to chase butterflies and listen to birds singing. Instead of eating mice, she would take cheese for them. One day, while rummaging through the trashcans, she found a bone with meat on it. "Why! This is sooo tasty!" she said in surprise. Just then, Gareth, the spotted puppy, woke up from his nap and saw Suzy chewing the bone. He thought, "Dogs are supposed to chew bones, not cats," and tried to snatch the bone. But Suzy would not let go off it. Gareth had an idea. He got a fish bone from the trashcan. When Suzy saw the fish bone, she left the bone she was licking and grabbed the fish bone. At once, Gareth pounced on the bone and ran off. But Suzy did not bother. After all, cats are supposed to enjoy fish bones more.

15   The Bee and Jupiter

One fine day, a queen bee flew up to Mount Olympus to make an offering of delicious honey to Jupiter, the Roman God of law and order. Graciously accepting her offer, Jupiter said, "I shall repay you for your devotion. Tell me your wish and I will grant it." The bee was greatly surprised. The queen bee's honey was so delicious that everybody would poke her honeycomb to extract honey. She had, therefore, for a long time wanted to teach these people a lesson. She promptly said to the God, "My Lord, kindly fill me with enough poison so that my sting can kill a person." Jupiter was in a great dilemma for he loved human beings and did not want to harm them. However, he could not forsake the promise. So he said, " shall fulfill your promise but it will cost you your life." That is why a bee dies after stinging.

16 The Fisherman and the Bear

After a fruitless day of fishing a fisherman returned home. The door of his house was open and a bear was eating his molasses! The fisherman shouted in anger and the bear ran out, its paw smeared with molasses. When the bear reached the lakeshore, flies attacked its sticky paw. The bear jumped into the lake and kept his paw above the water. Suddenly a big trout emerged and tried to get to the flies on the bear's paw but the bear brushed it aside and the trout went flying onto the shore. The bear threw several trout onto the shore. The fisherman had followed the bear. The bear saw him and decided to leave a few trout for him. The fisherman was very surprised. This was the first time a bear had repaid him for his molasses.

17 The Blue Duck

Mama Duck was swimming in the stream with her ducklings, Dinah, Dick and Derek. Dinah made faces at her brothers who were fighting. Mama told them to wait while she got them something to eat. In her absence, the brothers started fighting. Suddenly, Derek flew into the air and went away. When he returned, Mama was very angry and said, "Derek, if you fly too high your feathers will become blue and if you go near the clouds, your bill will become white. Wait here till I come back." But Derek did not pay attention to what his mother said. "Nothing will happen," he told his siblings. He took a deep breath and flew up to the sky. When he came back, Dinah and Dick cried out in surprise, "Derek, you've become blue and your bill has turned white! Mama was right!" Hearing the noise, Mama came running. When she saw Derek, she was very upset. Shamefaced, Derek went down to the pond to wash himself. Some duck hunters were near the pond. Hearing strange noises and seeing the weird creature they picked up their belongings and fled in terror. Derek had a hearty laugh. The blue colour never came off Derek's body but he had learnt his lesson and never disobeyed his mother.

18 Rainbow Crow

It had been a long cold winter. All the animals found it difficult to walk through the thick snow. In despair, the animals begged Rainbow Crow, the most beautiful bird with a beautiful voice, to go up to Heaven and beg God to stop the snow. Rainbow Crow pleaded to God to thaw the snow. God gave him a burning stick. But, by the time Rainbow Crow reached the Earth, his feathers had turned black due to the fire. His beautiful voice had become hoarse because of the smoke.

Meanwhile, the fire melted the snow and there was warmth and happiness on the Earth. God said to Rainbow Crow, "Don't be sad. Your black, smoky feathers will prevent men from hunting you and your hoarse voice will prevent them from putting you in a cage. So you will always be free and honoured for your sacrifice."

19 The Grasshopper and the Owl

There was once an owl who lived in a big oak tree. He slept during the day as all owls do. But the loud chirping of a grasshopper who lived in the flower bed below disturbed him. One day, he flew down to the grasshopper. "Friend Grasshopper, I have to stay awake at night to hunt for food. Your loud chirping disturbs my sleep. Will you be less noisy, please?" he requested.

The next day, the grasshopper chirped even louder. The owl decided to seek revenge. "I have a bottle of honey. Will you share it with me?" he invited the grasshopper. The greedy grasshopper went up to the owl's roost fluttering happily. Even before he could lay his hands on the honey, the owl grabbed him and put him inside the bottle. The grasshopper chirped and pleaded, but in vain. As for the owl—he slept peacefully from that day.

20 Playing Tricks

Fluffy, John and Weber waddled behind Mama Duck as she led them to the pond. "We'll learn swimming today!" quacked Fluffy and John. Weber, the naughty one, quickly slipped out and hid behind a bush. When they reached the pond, Mama Duck noticed Weber was missing and cried "Where's Weber?" Fluffy and John knew their brother well and said, "He must have been hiding again!" Mama asked them to wait while she went in search of Weber. Meanwhile, a huge gush of wind carried the two ducklings into the pond. They yelled for help. Mama came running and saw her ducklings struggling to stay afloat. She quickly rescued them. Suddenly they saw Weber approaching. "Your brothers were going to die because of your silly tricks," scolded Mama. Weber was really sorry and promised not to do it again.

21 Look Who's Sleeping

Linda was a little girl. She had lots of toys to play with. But she liked her teddies the most. There was a big teddy named Will and the three little ones named Wendy, Walter and Wesley. One day, she told them, "I am going out. You better behave." As soon as Linda left, the teddies started talking excitedly. "I am going to run and play in the garden!" said Wendy. "I will check the kitchen for honey!" said Walter. And all of them went jumping and dancing into the other room. Will was the strongest of them all. So he took all the toys for himself. When Wendy asked for the ball, he replied, "Go away." So the three little teddies left Will alone. Wesley ran into the kitchen and took out a wooden ladle and knocked all jars over. Wendy took Linda's wool and rolled it over. Suddenly they heard Linda's voice, "I am back!" All of them hurried back to bed and pretended to be sleeping.

Linda was shocked to see the mess. Everybody thought the cat must have done it and sent her out of the house for the day. The teddies winked at each other.

22 Nick the Mule Deer

While roaming in the woods, Nick, a baby mule deer, lost his way and was separated from his family. He began a frantic search in the woods and ran into Bossey the black bear. "I think they are in the farmer's field," said Bossey. Nick ran to the farmer's field but could not find anyone there. "Woof! Woof!" It was the farm dog. Nick turned to run. "Stop, stop, my friend," said the dog. He trotted up to Nick. "I am the watchdog. Why don't you stay with us?" he said. Nick accepted his offer and became friends with all the farm animals. Everyone in the farm loved Nick, but he still missed his family. One day, he noticed a huge herd of mule deer approaching the farm. There was his mother! Nick and his family were happily reunited. Nick thanked his new friends and promised to visit them again.

23 The Proud Eagle

On a bright, sunny day, a mighty eagle was soaring in the sky. Among the blue clouds, he lost touch with reality. He was very proud of his strength and thought, "I am the strongest and mightiest bird in the world. No one can harm me." Unknown to him, a bird catcher was following the flight of the eagle from the ground below. Suddenly, the eagle saw an arrow coming towards him. He tried to escape by flying as fast and high as he could. But alas! The arrow ripped through his body and he fell to the ground. He lay there bleeding and in pain. When he looked at the arrow that had pierced him, the eagle found that the shaft of the arrow was made of eagle feathers. "My foolish pride made me careless and has brought about my downfall." He decided to be more humble from that day onwards.

24 Snail Trail

Little Tina Snail was very upset on seeing her reflection in the water. "Oh! I am so ugly," she said terrified. She decided to leave the garden and live alone where no one could see her and laugh at her. She had barely gone a little way when she met two little earwigs. "Tina, we're so glad to find you. We're lost. Could you please help us to find our way home?" they asked Tina. "I wish they would go away," Tina mumbled to herself.

"Now we're safe," exclaimed one of the earwigs. "Tina's silver trail will sagely guide us home. It shines beautifully in the dark," said the other. The earwigs hopped home while Tina looked on, amazed. The silver trail she had made sparkled in the moonlight. "I didn't know that snail trails are so beautiful," said Tina with wonder. She realised that God blesses everyone with different kinds of beauty.

25 The Adventurous Rat

A family of rats lived in a burrow near a farmhouse. One of them, a lively young rat, grew tired of living in the dingy hole. One day, a relative came to visit them. Seeing the young rats, he urged their parents, "They can't learn anything about the world here. Let them explore the world!" The young rat was inspired by these words and wondered how beautiful the world outside would be. When everyone was asleep, he ventured out. Seeing the bright moon and the trees rustling in the soft breeze, he thought, "It's a beautiful world." The lights in the farmhouse were still on so the rat scurried in that direction. When he reached there, he found a number of people gathered around a table, laden with delicious food! The young rat's mouth watered. He noticed a room, full of utensils and food. "This must be the kitchen!" he thought and went inside. Suddenly he heard a woman cry, "This is the rat which nibbles at my food every day!" The young rat was baffled, "But this is only my first visit here," he thought. A young boy rushed in and said, "I shall tame him." He grabbed the rat's tail and locked him in a cage. So the young rat saw the world indeed but he was in a cage.

26 The Cat, the Partridge and the Hare

Once, there was a partridge who lived under a tree. One day, the partridge went looking for food. A hare who was passing by saw the empty home and decided to make it his own. Alas! When the partridge returned, he was shocked to see a hare in his house. He ordered the hare to leave the house but the hare said, "This place belongs to me since I'm living here now." Soon a fight broke out between them.

After a while, tired from fighting without any result, they took the matter to a cat who was a priest. This cat was very cunning. She decided to take advantage of them. "Ah," she licked her lips and said, "I can have a good dinner tonight." She sat under a tree at a distance and pretended to look very wise and closed her eyes. When the partridge and the hare complained about their problem, the cat pretended that she could not hear them. "I am becoming old day by day. I can't hear anything. You must come closer," she said gently. She bade them come nearer and nearer.

The partridge and the hare were so busy arguing with each other that they did not realise that the cat was very clever. They quickly went up to her and the cat opened her eyes, pounced on them and ate them up!

27   Why the Cheetah Runs Fast

Very long ago the cheetah was not a fast runner. He would chase other animals for food but often lost them because he could not run fast. He was sad and miserable. One day, he was wandering in the jungle in search of food when he came across a strange plant growing on the banks of a stream. The cheetah chewed the leaves of the plant and felt very thirsty. He lapped up water from the stream and lay beside it dreaming about food. Suddenly, he heard a faint noise and saw a boar in the distance. Feeling hungry, the cheetah chased the boar. And lo! He found himself running at a great speed. He was so excited that he forgot his hunger. The cheetah realised that the plant and stream were magical.

He took all his cheetah friends to that place and ever since cheetahs became the fastest creature on Earth.

28   The King of the Jungle

Larry the cub was scared of becoming the king of the jungle. His father said, "Larry, it's your destiny to become the king!" Larry ran away and hid in the jungle. Three monkeys saw him hiding and said, "Is that our future king? He's such a coward!" They threw fruits on his head and laughed. Larry started crying. Two toucans sitting on the tree above made fun of him and screeched in disgust, "Such behaviour is not acceptable from a future king." They too dropped sticky berries on his head. Poor Larry went to the river, crying and washed off the sticky fruit from his body. An ostrich passing by threw an egg at Larry.

This was too much for Larry! He roared in anger. All the animals ran away in fear. When his father heard this he was very happy and said, "You'll be a great king."

29 The Hawk and the Nightingale

One fine day, a nightingale was merrily singing in her nest. A hawk, who was flying overhead, heard the nightingale and stopped immediately. He flew down to a nearby tree and cast his evil eyes on the beautiful bird. "If she sings so beautifully," he thought, "I wonder how delicious her meat would be!" Without wasting another second he swooped down on the bird and carried her in his beak. The nightingale, who knew she was about to die, pleaded to the hawk to let her go, "Please let me go. Why should you have my meat when there are much bigger and better birds in the woods?" the hawk explained. "But I have you in my clutches! I am not foolish to let go off food which is already in my hand for the sake of food that is nowhere in sight."

30 A Game of Hide-and-Seek

Harry and Jack were two lion cubs. They enjoyed playing with their mother. One fine morning, Harry said, "Let us play hide-and-seek outside our den. Mama, you hide and we'll find you." Harry and Jack counted to ten and then went to look for her. Mama was nowhere to be seen! At last, Harry spotted her hiding in the bushes. Both of them crept up quietly from two sides and caught Mama by her arms. Now it was Mama's turn. She counted, "One, two...ten!" She saw them right away crouching behind the flowers but pretended she hadn't. "Did they hide in my gardening shed?" she said as she ran to the opening. Jack and Harry had fun watching their mama run all over the clearing.

Suddenly Mama surprised them from behind and grabbed them. They rolled over, laughing and giggling, while Mama tickled them with her nose.

31 The Man and the Serpent

A long long time ago, a farmer's son once accidentally stamped upon a serpent's tail. The serpent decided to take revenge and bit the little boy, who died at once. The farmer was enraged at his son's death. He took his axe and cut off a part of the serpent's tail. The serpent howled in pain and was again full of vengeance and decided to do something about it. He bit the farmer's cattle and caused the farmer great losses.

Now the farmer thought that it would be better to make peace with the serpent. One day, he took food and honey for him and said, "We have both taken our revenge, so let's forgive and forget and be friends now. Here, I have got some honey for you," the farmer offered.

But the serpent was not sure of the farmer's intention and looked at him suspiciously. He nodded his head in disagreement and said, "I do not think that is possible." The serpent told the farmer to take away his gifts and added, "As you cannot forget your son's death, I cannot forget that you've cut off my tail." Saying so, the serpent turned away and went into the forest.

Since then, men and serpents have been enemies.

Contents

The Story of the Month: The Big Leap

The Story of the Month

The Big Leap

01 The Big Leap

Toady the deaf frog lived with his friend, Froggy in a frog colony situated in a marsh near a big pit. The marsh was uninhabited by any snake or any other animals and the frogs led a happy, carefree life. Everyday, Toady and Froggy played with the other young frogs, hopping around from one leaf to another in the marsh.

Froggy was an adventurous young frog and always longed to see what lay inside the deep pit. "I want to hop into the pit and see what is there inside it," Froggy often told Toady. One day, while they were playing, Froggy said to Toady, "Today it's quite bright and sunny. Let's venture into the pit." "Croak!" said Toady who had strong faith in his friend's courage and they jumped into the dark pit. The other frogs saw Toady and Froggy jumping into the pit and croaked aloud, "Oh! What have they done? Don't they know that the pit is very deep!" They waited anxiously at the edge of the pit.

Meanwhile, inside the pit, Toady and Froggy landed on a rough surface. "It's so dark and dingy… I'm feeling scared," said Toady. Indifferent to Toady's fears, Froggy was busy looking

here and there and exploring. Suddenly, Froggy found some ants in a corner and shouted out loud to Toady who was hard of hearing, "Look! I've found a sumptuous meal."

Toady was trying hard to find a way out, for the pit was too deep to climb up or hop out. "Froggy!" shouted Toady with all his might. Quite startled at his friend's behaviour, Froggy looked up at Toady in the dark and asked, "What happened? Why do you look so annoyed?" Toady wore a serious look and said, "Froggy, I think we made a big mistake. I don't know how we will get back home." Hearing Toady, Froggy looked up for the first time and panicked. He also tried his best to hop out but all his attempts failed. All the frogs waiting outside shouted, "Oh, it's a pity! You won't be able to jump out." Their words made Froggy lose all his courage and he gasped for breath. Feeling lost and suffocated, Froggy was in tears.

Deaf Toady could not hear what the other frogs were saying. He thought they were encouraging him to climb up. Toady mustered all his courage and took a big leap and lo! He was out of the pit. Everyone clapped and cheered for Toady.

Toady then thought of an idea and got a rope and helped Froggy come out of the pit. The two frogs decided never to go near the pit again.

02 A Cat and Mouse Game

Bruce was a mouse that lived in Mr. Bairdie's house. He was very fond of cheese. One day, Bruce was feeling hungry and thought, "Let me explore the kitchen." There he saw a box on the counter which was stuffed with lots of crackers, biscuits and cheese! Bruce's eyes shone with happiness. "Everything looks so tasty!" he squeaked and picked up a biscuit. But he found them very salty. Bruce then decided to try the cheese instead. "Yummy! Just what I like!" he said . In the same house there also lived a cat named Callum who had been watching Bruce. "Ah, I have let Bruce get fat, now I must eat him!" he thought and pounced on Bruce. Bruce ran to his hole but couldn't get in! He had eaten so much that he was too fat for the tiny hole! Finally, he managed to squeeze through and ran into his hole with great effort. At night, he dreamt of lots of cats chasing him. He woke up panting with fear. "I will never ever eat so much again!" he promised himself.

03 Brer Rabbit Falls down the Well

One day, Brer Rabbit, Brer Fox and Brer Bear were working in a field. It was a hot day and Brer Rabbit thought, "Maybe I can take a tiny nap." He pretended that a thorn had pricked his paw and went to a nearby well to wash it. He saw a bucket hanging over the well and thought, "What a nice place to rest." He jumped into the bucket. Whooosh… down he went into the well! Sly Brer Fox had followed Brer Rabbit. On seeing Brer Fox, Brer Rabbit called out, "There are lots of fish in this well! Why don't you jump into the other bucket?" As soon as Brer Fox got in, Brer Rabbit's bucket went up. He jumped out of the well and ran back to the field, while poor Brer Fox was stuck crying for help!

04 The Lost Whale

One day while swimming, Bubbles the young blue whale, swam far away from home. Suddenly, a storm swept over him and he was carried to an unknown place. The wild seas made him twist and turn and he felt sick. None of his friends, the octopus, the jellyfish or the tuna was there. Bubbles felt lonely and sad. He swam alone trying to find a way back home. He heard a faint whistle. He tossed up into the air and saw a faraway ship. When the ship approached nearer, he waved to the captain and said, "Could you please show me the way?" "Follow me," said the kind captain. Bubbles followed the trail of the ship and came back home after a while where his friends were waiting for him eagerly. As he embraced his friends, he swore never to swim away into unknown waters.

05 Families

A Papa Bear, Mama Bear and Baby Bear named Bobby were hibernating in a cave. "When will we go outside the cave?" Bobby asked Mama Bear impatiently.

She replied, "Tomorrow. It is spring and we shall go out as a family." The next morning, all the three bears wore their best clothes. Bobby was very excited as he would be going out of the cave for the first time! While walking in the woods, Bobby asked, "What is a family?" Mama Bear said, "In a family, there is a papa, a mama and a baby." Bobby saw a mama raccoon and her babies. He was puzzled and he asked, "How come there is no papa with them?" Mama Bear explained that sometimes there may be no papa or mama but it is still a family. That night, kissing his mama good night Bobby said, "Mama, a family is wherever love is."

06 The Cat and the Dog

Many years ago, there lived an old man with his son and daughter-in-law. They were very poor but they were happy. Before he died, the old man gave his daughter-in-law three gold coins. Now the son and his wife were left alone.

One day there was no food in the house. The wife gave the man one gold coin and asked him to buy food. He went to the market but instead of buying food he bought a cat. The wife said nothing. She cooked whatever little food there was and they all shared the food. The next day, the wife gave another gold coin to him. This time the man brought home a stray dog that some children had been teasing. Sometime later, the wife fell ill and the third gold coin was spent. The dog said to the man, "Master, we want to help you." "How can you help me?" said the man. "O' Master, the cat knows of a magical dragon stone. We will find that stone." The next day, the dog and the cat set off on their mission. They had to face many obstacles on their way. At last they found the stone. The two friends quickly brought out the magical stone and took it back home. The stone fulfilled all their wishes and they were never poor again.

07 Naughty Kitty

Mrs. Zowski had a cat named Tiger who was very clever. One day, Mrs. Zowski had to go to her friend's house. She said, "Now Tiger, don't be naughty. There is food in your plate, okay?" For a while, Tiger behaved himself. Then he wondered, "What should I do now? Let me check the cupboards." Tiger found chocolates and ate them all, throwing the wrappers in front of the mouse hole. Then he saw the goldfish in the aquarium. "Yummy!" said Tiger and gobbled them up. Then he went to sleep. Meanwhile, Mrs. Zowski returned and found the aquarium empty and the wrappers in front of the mouse hole. She cried, "Who ate my fish and chocolates?" Tiger pointed to the mouse hole. Mrs. Zowski said, "Oh, the mouse did! Did you eat the mouse?" Tiger rubbed his tummy. "Good kitty, Tiger!" said Mrs. Zowski and Tiger purred mischievously.

08   How the Alligator Got Its Teeth

Around a hundred years ago, in a pond, there lived a cruel and greedy alligator. He would hide in the rushes or in the mud and lie in wait for his victim. In those days alligators did not have any teeth. The alligator used to gobble up whole any living creature that came to drink water in the pond. One day, as the alligator was swallowing another animal, a chipmunk came along to drink water. The alligator got greedy. He thought, "Today I will eat to my fullest. First, I shall eat this animal and then I will eat that chipmunk." Alas! The alligator did not see that the chipmunk was sitting on a thorny bush. As the alligator swam towards the chipmunk with wide open jaws, he bumped into the thorny bush. All the thorns stuck in his mouth and they hardened to become his teeth.

Since then, all alligators have teeth.

09   Where Is the Rain?

Once there were two birds called Pooky and Sooky. One day, Pooky said, "It is so hot! I really wish it would rain soon." Sooky replied, "Yes, all the grass is turning brown and even the ponds are getting dry." Both the birds were thirsty. They flew hither and thither in search of water. Suddenly Pooky exclaimed, "Look, Sooky—water! Let's drink water from this pond." But Sooky warned him, "Wait! I can see a big alligator. It looks dangerous." So they flew ahead but couldn't find any river or pond. Finally tired, they fell asleep on a branch. Suddenly, there was a thundering sound. Alarmed, they both woke up to see big black clouds overhead. "Hurrah! It is going to rain," said Pooky. And the rain came pouring down. Soon all the rivers, ponds and puddles were full of water. The two birds were happy and splashed around in the rain.

10 Rufus and Tutu Grow Up

Once, there was a Mama Bear who had two little cubs, Rufus and Tutu. They were very naughty and spent all their time playing. They never went with Mama Bear to collect honey or berries.

One day Mama Bear thought, "This way they will never learn to hunt on their own. I must teach them to get their own food." So she thought of a clever plan. She climbed up a tree and pretended to sleep. After a while, Rufus came and looked up, "Mama, I am hungry!" Mama Bear pretended not to hear and kept her eyes closed. Then Tutu came, "Mama, I am thirsty!" But Mama Bear kept on sleeping. "What should we do?" cried Tutu. They were very worried. Now, both of them realised that they would have to get their own food. After that day, they never troubled Mama Bear again.

11 Mikoo's Jungle Picnic

One day, Mikoo the frog invited his best friends Kallu the crow, Mimi the monkey, and Lola the lioness for a picnic.

Mikoo was very excited. They would go to the riverside and spread a nice white sheet on the grass. Then Mikoo would share sandwiches and sweets with all his friends. What fun it was going to be! Mikoo could hardly wait.

When his friends arrived, Mikoo spread out all the tasty treats. Suddenly Mikoo had a lot of uninvited guests—ants! And oh, so many of them! Mikoo had to cancel the picnic while the ants feasted on the delicious food. Poor Mikoo was nearly in tears. He decided never to have a picnic in the forest again.

12 The Horse, the Hunter and the Stag

There lived two friends, a horse and a stag, in a jungle. One day, they quarrelled and the stag went away. The horse got angry at the stag and thought to himself, "I will take revenge." He ran but could not catch up with the swift stag. Finally, the horse decided to take a hunter's help. The hunter was very smart. He told the horse that they both would run faster if the horse allowed the hunter to saddle him. The horse believed the hunter. As soon as the hunter sat on the horse, they galloped fast and soon overtook the stag. The hunter shot the stag. The shocked horse asked the hunter to get off him. But the hunter replied, "Now you are my slave and you have to listen to my commands." The horse learned a hard lesson that day, "If you allow anyone to use you for your own purposes, then they will take advantage of you."

13 William the Wasp

One day, William the wasp buzzed into an open kitchen. He caught delicious smells as he zipped around the kitchen inspecting the jars. "Ooh sugar!" he said and took a taste of it. Then he saw a jar of honey in the cupboard. Honey was William's favourite. He flew to the bottle. Just then the cupboard door went "Bang!" William felt lost in the dark but he managed to squeeze out through a crack. "Free at last!" he thought gleefully to himself.

The lady in the kitchen saw William and started waving her arms. "Wasp! Out! Out!" she shouted chasing him with a rolled-up newspaper. Seeing a dog enter the kitchen, William dove down and hid in the dog's fur. Feeling tickled, the dog rolled on the floor and scratched himself and ran out in the garden. Hurriedly, William flew into the garden and vowed never to go back again!

14 Malmo the Wounded Rat

Sam Tills was a lonely man. He worked in a cotton mill. Each morning he would go to work and in the evening he would walk back home, alone. One day while returning home, he found a white rat lying in the middle of the road. At first he thought that the rat was dead. Sam went up to the rat and saw that it was still alive—only its leg was broken. He took it home. He named his little rat, Malmo. Sam fed the rat and played with him daily. At night, he gently stroked Malmo's fur to make him go to sleep. Soon both became friends. Sam carried Malmo in his hat to the mill. Even on Sundays, when Sam visited his sister's house, he took Malmo along. When Sam sang, Malmo would sleep on his master's head. Now Sam was no longer lonely because he had someone to love.

15 Bruno the Busy Dog

Bruno was Tim's pet dog. He was not lazy like most other dogs. He woke up early in the morning to pick up the milk bottles and newspaper kept at the door. He accompanied Tim's mother to the market and helped her carry a basket. One day Bruno, decided to have some fun. "I need a break now!" he thought while he watched other dogs playing in the park. So he went to Tim's father and asked him if he would play. "I am busy working on something," explained Tim's father. Bruno then went to Tim. "Bruno, I have to finish this assignment!" said Tim. Bruno went to the garden and asked a butterfly to play with him. "Sorry Bruno, but I am visiting a new garden to-day," replied the butterfly. Nobody was free to play with Bruno. Just then, Tim's mother called out, "Bruno, come here!" "Wow! She wants to play with me." thought Bruno and rushed to the kitchen. "I am keeping some fish here. Keep a watch on it while I am away," she said. "Ah! At least I have something to do, it's better than sitting idle," thought Bruno and stood guard near the fish.

16 The Tortoise and the Eagle

A long time ago, there lived a tortoise by the sea. Every day, he would swim in the sea and then bask in the sun. When he lay down, he would complain, "Ah, my friends! How useless my life is! I would enjoy my life more if I could fly in the air! I wish someone would teach me how to fly!" An eagle heard the tortoise. He said, "If I teach you, what will you give me?" The tortoise was happy to hear this. He said, "I will give you all the riches of the Red Sea." The eagle took the tortoise to a great height and dropped him. The tortoise came tumbling down and hit a hard rock. The tortoise mumbled in pain, "I am responsible for my state. I should have been happy with what God had given me."

17 Brer Rabbit Rides a Fox

Brer Rabbit loved to boast. One day, he was bragging to Mrs. Meadows, "My grandfather used to ride a fox for a horse!" "Oh really!!" said Mrs. Meadows. That day, Mrs. Meadows told the fox about him. The fox decided to teach the rabbit a lesson. He went to the rabbit's burrow and yelled, "Come out!" Brer Rabbit knew the fox was angry, so he called back, "Oh, Mr. Fox, I am so ill. Will you please carry me to the doctor on your back?" The fox thought that the rabbit was really ill and agreed. Brer Rabbit sat on the fox's back and glided past the house showing Mrs. Meadows how he rode a fox. Suddenly, the fox realised his mistake. He ran so fast that Brer Rabbit fell down. Brer Rabbit quickly got up and hid in a tree hollow. The fox waited outside. Meanwhile, a turkey passed by and the fox asked him to watch the rabbit for he needed to do some work. The rabbit saw the turkey guarding the hollow. He thought for a while and said loudly, "There is a squirrel in the hollow that would make a tasty meal for a turkey. I will push it out from the other side." When the turkey heard this, he went around. Brer Rabbit jumped out of the hole and ran away.

18   Why the Vulture is Bald

Long, long ago, the vulture had feathers. But he was very sad and wished his feathers were as beautiful as the peacock's. He would crib about his simple feathers all the time. The other birds took pity and decided to contribute their feathers to make him look exquisite. Soon the vulture became the prettiest bird. But alas! He became proud of his new look and often misbehaved with his peers. So the other bids pecked off his feathers and made him bald and ugly, like he is today!

19   Cedric the Pig

Cedric the pig loved to spend the whole day in the mud pit. The stickier the mud was, all the better for Cedric! He loved to be covered neck deep in mud. His friends never saw him leave that spot. He never hunted for food as he feared some other pig might take his place. If any of the pigs wanted to use the mud pit, they had to shoulder Cedric away to get a place for themselves. Nobody knew that Cedric hunted for food at night when all the others slept. He would eat his fill so that he would not feel hungry during the day.

One day, it rained so hard that Cedric had to leave his mud pit. As he stood in the rain, all the mud covering his body was washed away. His skin changed from muddy brown to glowing pink. When Cedric returned, the others were just coming out of the pen. They stared at Cedric and though he grunted and oinked, nobody recognised him. "It's me, Cedric," he said. "No, you're not!" said Patrick. Cedric tried his best to convince Patrick and the other pigs but failed. "Cedric never leaves the pit," said one of the other pigs. "Just follow me and see," said Cedric going towards the mud pit. Cedric jumped into the muddy pool and became brown and sticky once more. He rolled around and let the mud slather him to his heart's content. "It is Cedric, after all," oinked Patrick and the other pigs in surprise.

20 The Clean Elephant

James the elephant was different from other animals. When all the animals were having fun playing in the mud, James would sit alone. Unlike the others, he hated getting dirty. One day, due to heavy showers, there was mud everywhere. James too became dirty and the mud was caked all over his body. "Oh no! I just cleaned my toenails this morning," grumbled James to himself. When the rain stopped, James saw all the animals bathing in the river. "Oh! I cannot bathe here! It is too dirty!" he thought. He went to the waterfall but it was muddy there too. The rhino called out to him, "Come, James! The water feels good!" As soon as James stepped into the river, all the mud was washed away. He found himself having fun with his friends. From that day onwards, he bathed and played along with all the other animals of the jungle.

21 The Crafty Cat

Thomas the cat lived in a small town. He had eaten all the rats there. He wondered, "What now? I have nothing to eat." Finally, he went to live in the fields. He sat under a tree, with a rosary in his hand and pretended to meditate. After a few hours, a tiny rat came out of his hole and asked him, "What are you doing, Sir?" "I am praying. I don't eat rats anymore," Thomas said. The rat went back and told his family. The rats decided to test him. An elderly rat came out of the hole and scampered about. Thomas ignored him. This went on for sometime. Soon, Thomas grew hungry and thought, "Enough of this. I will eat this rat." But as soon as he moved, the rat ran back into his hole. The cat's plan failed and he was forced to leave the field.

22 The Greedy Crow

Once there was a pigeon who lived in her nest near the kitchen window of a palace. The royal cooks would feed her grain and breadcrumbs every day. One day, a crow saw the pigeon eating grain. He thought, "Ah! If I stay with her then I will also get food." Soon they became good friends and the crow persuaded the pigeon to share her nest with him. But the pigeon made it clear that when it came to food, they would have to find their own. The crow was unhappy about this and thought, "Let me go directly into the kitchen! There I can get a variety of food." He flew in through the window and saw fish in the pan. But as he was about to take it, he dropped the ladle. The cooks woke up and spanked the crow. That was how the poor crow got punished because of his greed.

23 The Mongoose and the Brahmin's Wife

A Brahmin named Devasarman and his wife did not have any children. So they adopted a mongoose as their son. Soon the family was blessed with a baby boy. The wife continued to love the mongoose as much as her own son. One day, she went out to fetch water from the well. In her absence, a big snake entered the house and slithered slowly towards the baby boy who was sleeping in his cot. When the mongoose saw this, he pounced on the snake and killed him. The mongoose was happy that he had saved his brother. But when the wife came in, she saw blood on the mongoose's lips and yelled, "Oh, you foolish animal, you have killed my son!" She beat the mongoose with a stick and drove it into the forest. When she went inside and saw the dead snake, she realised her mistake. She wept with sorrow but it was too late.

24 The Brazier and His Lazy Dog

Once, there was a hardworking brazier who used to make beautiful brass articles. He had a very lazy dog. While the brazier worked, the dog would laze around, doing nothing. But as soon as his master sat down to eat, the dog would come up to him, wagging his tail and begging for food. This was the dog's daily routine. One day, the dog slept the whole day and when his master sat for his meal, he woke up and ran to him. The brazier ignored the dog but the dog kept nudging his master. The master was really angry and yelled, "You wretched little sluggard! You have no right to eat food! You never work and food should always be served to those who work for it." The dog learned his lesson well. From that day onwards he helped his master in whatever way he could.

25 The Frogs and the Crane

Deep in the forest was a pond. In the pond lived a big colony of frogs. In the moonlight, all the frogs would sit on the shore and set up a chorus of croaking. Some of the voices would be deep, some would be shrill and still others, somewhere in-between. The deep voices belonged to the bullfrogs who were always competing among themselves. The first frog bragged, "I am the chief of the pond." The second one also said the same, followed by the third one. While they were trying to outdo each other, a big crane came along. He picked up the first frog in his beak. But as he was about to gobble the frog, he saw a small water snake at his feet. The crane grabbed the snake instead. The frog escaped as fast as he could. The next day, the crane went to eat the second frog. At the last moment, he saw a mink that was hoping to catch him and the crane quickly flew away to the farthest bank. The second frog was saved but he never croaked again. He quietly returned to the pond. The next day, the crane caught hold of the third frog's leg and was going to gulp him when a fox chanced by and chased the crane. The crane had to let go off the frog. The third frog quickly hopped away to safety. The three frogs had had a narrow escape. They had also learnt an important lesson: never to brag!

26 Why Do Kangaroos Hop?

Kip was a little baby kangaroo. He was a very naughty kangaroo and was always full of questions.

One day, Kip went to his mother and asked, "Mama, why do I hop? Why can't I fly or swim or slide on my belly?" Mama smiled and replied, "We are kangaroos and meant to hop like that." But Kip was not satisfied, so he hopped to the nearby pond to meet his friends.

Near the pond, he met his friend, Kimmy the koala bear. "Kimmy, do you hop?" asked Kip. Kimmy said, "No, Kip. I don't know how to hop. But I can climb trees." Then Kip asked Cedric the crocodile why he swam. Cedric was a very wise crocodile. He replied, "I can swim. I can't climb trees or hop or run. That is how it is meant to be."

Kip realised that every creature has its own strengths and that he was also special as he could hop and nobody else could do that.

27 Skippity and Hippity

Skippity Rabbit was worried. "Why do I get all these thoughts? I always think of things like, why is the sky blue, why are rabbits and snow of the same colour and why did Mrs. McGregor make a pie out of Peter Rabbit!" he wondered. Skippity went to his sister, Hippity for finding the answers to all his questions. She was the smartest bunny he had ever come across. "Why is she so smart?" he thought again.

Hippity Rabbit always read a lot of books. She said, "There are so many questions in my mind, you know. I want to find answers to all my questions. I find that when I read books, I find an answer to almost every question I think of." She suggested, "Maybe you should also read, Skippity." From that day onwards, Skippity also read his sister's books.

28   The Eagle and the Owl

The owl and the eagle signed a treaty that they wouldn't eat each other's babies. The eagle asked, "How will I recognise your babies?" "They will be the prettiest," replied the Mother Owl. One day, the hungry eagle was flying over a clump of trees when he saw a nest of ugly, screeching little baby birds. "These strange looking birds could never be baby owls," the eagle thought to himself. He swooped down and ate them all. The owl was grief-stricken when she returned. But who can blame the eagle? He did not realise that to every mother her child is the best!

29   Windy Day

It was a windy day. Grandma Bear and her little grandson, Pipkin were busy hanging the washed clothes on the clothesline. Just then the telephone rang and Grandma Bear rushed to answer it. The wind was so strong that it tugged at the hooks holding the clothes. Pipkin was very worried. He called Grandpa Bear and lo! As soon as Grandpa arrived, a white sheet flew off the line and wrapped it-self around him. Pipkin tried to untangle Grandpa, but the sheet clung to his body firmly. Grandma came out and saw the white figure. "Help! It's a ghost!" she screamed and began running away as fast as she could. "Stop! Stop! It's me…your loving husband!" said Grandpa anxiously. Grandma replied nodding her head, "Grandpa, you are too old to play games like this. Keep still while I untangle this mess!" She then took the sheet to wash it again.

30   Defeated by Pride

Once upon a time, two roosters challenged each other to a fight to see who was stronger of the two. The two fought for hours and hours. After the fight, the loser hid himself behind some bushes, sulking at his defeat. The winner flew to the roof and proudly declared, "I've won! I've won! I'm the best." Suddenly an eagle swooped down and carried away the proud rooster. The other rooster peeped from behind the bushes and saw the eagle taking him away. Soon, he became the master of the farmyard. The moral of the story is too much pride leads to one's downfall.

Contents

The Story of the Month: Helping Hands

The Story of the Month

Helping Hands

01 Helping Hands

Burton the beaver was watching the tossing waves of a river flooded by heavy rains. Suddenly, he spotted a tortoise struggling in the gushing water. He quickly jumped into the river and swam across. He asked the tortoise to climb on his back and swam along with the flow of the current towards the bank. "Thank you for saving my life," said the tortoise. "My name is Torquil. Who are you?" "I am Burton." As Burton glided through the muddy water, Torquil noticed a pile of feathers and asked, "What is that?"

Burton moved closer and they found Rose, a red-breasted robin, being tossed about in the water. Torquil quickly grabbed its tail and pulled it on its back. Completely drenched in the floodwater, the little bird shivered and coughed a soft, "Thank you." "Do not worry, I saved Torquil too," said Burton and cautiously swam across the swirling water.

As Rose sat on Torquil's back, she noticed a tiny red object fighting to stay afloat. "Over there, over there!" she exclaimed. Burton swam as fast as he could.

On arriving, the three sighed aloud. It was the most beautiful creature they had ever seen—a red-bodied insect with black polka dots. It was a little ladybird!

Burton asked the ladybird to jump on. Now safely perched, the ladybird introduced herself. "I am Lindsey." Examining Rose's bright red feathers, she said, "You are a pretty bird, but none here is as beautiful as I am." Burton replied, "Do not be so vain. Each of us is beautiful in our own way." The four continued their journey.

Burton exclaimed, "This journey is so exciting. We can see such beautiful creations of God!" Lindsey, who at a greater height could see inside the lilac petals, saw a struggling insect and said, "Oh, that creature needs a helping hand." Rose quickly flew down with Lindsey on her back and grabbed the lilac branch with her beak. As they placed it on Torquil's hard shell, out popped a pretty butterfly. With a warm smile it said, "Thank you everybody for saving my life. My name is Bonnie."

As the sun set, Burton realised he would have to halt for the night. The river water had started receding. Burton spotted a rock in the water. It was big enough for all five of them. "It's time for me to go and gather pollen from the flowers. Thank you for everything," said Bonnie. Saying this, she flew away. One by one, everybody said goodbye and went on their way. When it was time for Torquil to leave, he said, "I am feeling rather safe on your back and would like to stay with you and help you build your home." Burton happily agreed and the two swam down the now calm river.

02 Two Old Friends

It was a bright sunny morning in the highlands of Scotland. Catriona, the highland sheep, saw her friend, Bruce the spider and said, "It's been such a long time since I have met my friend, Nessie, who stays in the Loch Ness. Would you come with me to meet her?" Bruce jumped at the offer of seeing an animal he had only heard about in legends. As they climbed down the mountain they saw Angus the bull and asked him to join them. On their way, they met a few more friends—Malcolm the dog, Fiona the grouse and Duncan the pony. All of them were very eager to see Nessie. As they neared their destination, their excitement grew. On reaching the lake Catriona called out loud, "Nessie, I have come with my friends to meet you." A huge monster emerged from the quiet waters. It was green in colour, with clawlike teeth and a long neck. "Where are your friends, Catriona?" asked Nessie. She turned to find all of them hiding behind a bush! Though scared, the animals came out and touched Nessie's rough skin. They asked her if she was a monster. "How does it matter who I am, as long as we are friends?" said Nessie. She invited all the animals on her back and showed them the lake. They were delighted. As the sun began to set, it was time for everyone to return home. Catriona and her friends bade Nessie a sad goodbye, promising to return soon.

03 Warm Paws and Ears

Winter was at its peak. Huge snowflakes were falling from the sky and everything was covered with snow. Amidst the heavy snow, Claire the hare with long ears, large paws and a fluffy tail was hopping around. She was very hungry. She wondered, "Why do the winters come? There are no radishes to eat. I wish I had some food." Tired of hunting, Claire returned to her burrow, where it was cosy and warm. "What do I do now?" she thought. Suddenly, Claire had an idea. She would knit warm woollen clothes! So she started knitting. When she finished knitting, she had a small pair of socks to warm her paws and earmuffs to keep her long ears warm. Now she was ready to face the snow and hunt for food.

04 Selfish Penny

Peter, Pan and Penny were three sea birds who lived on a cliff near the sea. Penny grew tired of going back and forth to collect fish from the sea. So she told her brothers, "Since I am the eldest, the two of you will collect fish for me every day." Though unhappy with the decision, Peter and Pan religiously flew down from the cliff and scooped out fish from the sea. It was a difficult task. After each round, their strength gradually decreased and they often failed to scoop out any fish. This continued for some days and one day, both Peter and Pan refused to give any fish to Penny. "Don't be lazy. Go and get the fish yourself," they told Penny. Now Penny had no alternative but to fly down to get her own food.

05 Three Hungry Rats

Three rats, Wiggles, Twitch and Fluffy lived among a pile of rocks. While Wiggles and Twitch were small, Fluffy was big and fat. All the three were good friends and spent the day playing and hunting for food together. Soon, winter set in and finding food became very difficult. Wiggles and Twitch became weak and asked Fluffy to help them get food. Fluffy finally agreed. He said, "Don't be surprised if I do not return because those hungry cats and foxes are also looking for food." While crossing the fields, Fluffy saw smoke rising from the chimney of a house. "Something smells good!" he sniffed. He hurried towards the house and jumped in through the window. "Zzzz…" Fluffy's heart skipped a beat. He saw a cat sleeping in the middle of the room. He quickly scampered behind a sofa. Mustering courage, Fluffy crept into the kitchen and saw a cheese casserole on the table. He had first picked it up when he heard "Sppptt!" Turning back, he found the cat, ready to pounce. Fluffy jumped out of the window with the cat behind him. Luckily, he found a haystack and hid inside it. The cat meowed angrily and after a while went back. Fluffy came out of the haystack and ran home with the casserole. His friends were relieved to see him. They nibbled on the delicious treat and thanked God that their friend was still alive.

06 The Vain Mouse

Silvia thought that she was the prettiest mouse in the world. All day long, she looked at herself in the river. "Oh! Such a great complexion, such beautiful whiskers and what a fine-looking tail I have!" she would exclaim. One fine day, a leaf fell in the river creating ripples. Unable to see herself, Silvia ran into a stable where she found a horse drinking water from a bucket.

When the horse had finished, Silvia jumped onto the bucket. Seeing a mouse on his bucket, the horse gave it a kick and Silvia fell into the bucket. Terribly frightened, she jumped out and fled inside the farmer's house. Here, she found a bowl of water and again began preening herself. Seeing a dirty drenched mouse, the farmer's wife shrieked. She ran with a broom to kill it.

Silvia ran for her life and swore never to be so vain.

07 The Boar's Foresight

Once upon a time, there lived a hardworking boar and a very lazy fox in a jungle.

One day, the boar was rubbing his tusk against a tree. Just then, the fox passed by and became curious as to what the boar was doing. He asked, "Hey, friend! What are you doing?" The boar replied, "I am sharpening my tusk. This is my weapon to defend myself against enemies!" The fox laughed at the boar

and said, "But there is no danger right now! Why are you troubling yourself like this? I think you are wasting time."

Just then, a hunter spotted the two animals. He raised his gun to shoot them. The fox stood still with fear but the boar gave charge. Seeing the sharp tusk of the boar, the hunter fled.

The fox thanked the boar for saving his life and said, "Thank you, friend. Now I know that it is always better to be prepared for danger!"

08 Clever Mrs. Rabbit

Mr. and Mrs. Sandy Rabbit and their family lived inside a draughty hole near sand dunes. When winters approached Mrs. Rabbit said, "We need a warmer dwelling." So Mrs. Rabbit went to meet her friend, Mrs. Duck "Will you buy our hole?" she asked. Mrs. Duck said, "I will and in exchange you can have a bag of my family's soft down. It will keep you warm." When she returned home Mr. Rabbit was very angry. "We will all die of cold without our hole," he declared. Mrs. Rabbit returned the down sadly. Suddenly, an idea struck her. Everyday, she combed her family and collected their fur. Soon she wove a big blanket with it. Now the Rabbit family could protect themselves from the harsh winter. And they didn't have to leave their home too. All because of clever Mrs. Rabbit!

09 Sam the Seahorse

Fish are colourful. Some have patches or stripes, while others have brilliant, shiny bodies. They can blow bubbles and swim quickly in water. However, there was one, who was very different from all the rest. His name was Sam and he was a seahorse. He did not have bright patches on his body. He floated in one place most of the time with his tail wrapped around seaweed. The other fish often made fun of his long snout and his funny grin. "Look at Sam," they would whisper. "He hardly moves about!" Sam tried not to let their comments bother him but he felt sad and lonely. Then one day, a school of fish swam by Sam and saw him smiling happily. "What's up with Sam," said an angelfish in surprise. "I have never seen him smile before," added a clown fish. The fish swam closer to Sam and saw a cluster of tiny seahorses popping out from Sam's pouch! "What's that?" they asked curiously. "These are my babies and I take care of them!" said Sam. "The mother is supposed to look after babies," said the fish. "Not if you're a seahorse. Seahorse fathers look after their babies," explained Sam patiently.

All the other fish swam around admiring the seahorse babies. They praised Sam for being a caring father. "We would love to come and visit you and the babies," said the fish. From that day, the other fish helped Sam look after the babies and became his friends.

10 Reaching for the Sky

In a field next to an apple orchard lived two bunnies, two bears, two chicks, a cow, a cat and a mouse. Every year, they waited for the spring to arrive when apples appeared on the trees. Sometimes when few apples fell on the ground, they sneaked in to steal them. To teach the animals a lesson, the owner of the orchard cut off the lower branches of the trees.

"Oh no!" sighed the group of animals. "I will miss the juicy apples," sighed one bear. The cat, who was the most intelligent in the group, had a plan. He said that they could all relish apples if they followed his plan. One by one, he made each animal stand on top of the other to form a pyramid. The mouse, who was right on top, quickly plucked the apples. Later, they sat together and enjoyed the delicious fruit.

11 Feeding the Ducks

One fine morning, Maggie and her grandfather went down to the lake to feed the ducks. Maggie had a bag full of breadcrumbs. When they neared the lake, Grandpa said to her, "Child, reach out and throw the breadcrumbs into the lake." All the ducks quacked out loud and fought over the breadcrumbs. As they picked up the crumbs with their long orange beaks, Grandpa showed Maggie the different kinds of ducks. Some ducks had green-coloured rings around their necks. "Those are the male Mallard ducks, while the ones with a brown ring are females," said Grandpa. When Maggie held out her bag and called out to the ducks, one duck quickly came, stretched out and pulled the bag out of her hands! Maggie was disappointed. Soon it began to rain and Maggie and Grandpa had to return home.

12   The Dragon's Soup

One day, a hungry dragon wanted to make some soup. He lit the firewood and placed a pot of water over it. A flock of birds, that happened to see the boiling water, realised that the dragon was making soup. They asked if they could have some soup to eat. "Only if you get something to put in it," said the dragon. At once, the birds went out to collect the ingredients. After a while, one returned with a snake, another with a duck egg, some with mushrooms and carrots, while others brought lizards and frogs. The dragon asked them to drop everything in the pot. Once the soup was cooked, the dragon gave each bird a bowl of soup. The dragon then had a big bowl of soup and said that it was the best soup he had ever had.

13   The Big Egg

Chipo was a very naughty monkey. One day, while plucking bananas from a tree, he saw a huge egg lying nearby. Chipo quickly went to meet his friends, Juma the tiger cub and Zina and Pemba the twin ants. He told them about his great discovery. At first they brushed aside Chipo's story, but when he described the egg, their curiosity grew too. A bumblebee heard them and told Chipo that he too wanted to see the egg. Zaid the snake, heard the commotion and came out from his hole. Finally, Chipo and his team of friends set off to the tree where the egg lay. All the animals were amazed at the size. While the animals were busy examining the egg, a voice shrieked, "What are you ruffians doing to my egg?" They turned back startled. They saw a huge bird with long, sturdy legs! It had fluffy feathers on its long neck. "Who are you?" they squeaked together. "I am an ostrich and this is my egg," said the bird angrily. "Go away or else I shall kill you," she warned. All the animals ran away in fear.

14 Read or Play

Kenny the elephant, loved to read. All day long, he would lock himself in his room and read books on different subjects. His mother scolded him for not eating his food on time and for not going out to play. "Go and pick up the log and water the plants!" she told Kenny one day.

Reluctantly, Kenny went along with his mother into the garden. While he lifted the log and sprayed the plants, he noticed that his mother was keeping a strict watch on him. Tears welled up in his eyes while Kenny finished the task. When he returned, his mother said, "I know you love to read, so I will not ask you to lift logs or water the plants, but you must at least eat your food." Kenny smiled and hugged his mother.

Later, he ate his food and went back to read his favourite books.

15 The Pink Balloon

Every spring, a big children's fair is organised at Panda Park. Many people visit this fair. There are ice cream and pastry shops, candy floss vendors, carousels and giant wheels at the fair. Young boys play drums and pipes while some dress up as clowns and perform various tricks.

One day, Terry the brown bear, went to visit the fair. The colourful balloons in a shop caught his attention. He found the balloon seller making various shapes out of them. He saw a huge pink balloon and asked the man if he could buy it. The shopkeeper said it was bigger in size than Terry, so he should buy the blue one instead. Terry refused to listen and bought the pink one. However, the balloon was too big for Terry. He lost control and the balloon soared into the sky. The shopkeeper gave him the blue one and Terry felt better.

16   How to Catch Fish

One winter morning, Mama Polar Bear took her cubs, Snowball and Icicle, to a lake to teach them fishing. Once there, Icicle asked, "Mama, how can we catch fish? The lake is covered with ice." Mama Polar Bear explained that even though the water had turned into ice, one could still find fish in places. She took them across to a place where the ice was thin and brittle. Placing her heavy paws over it, she crushed the ice and made a hole. Snowball peered into it and was amazed to find clear blue water beneath! Mama Polar Bear slipped through the hole into the water. Seeing their mama going inside the hole, the cubs grew anxious. They started crying for her, when out popped their mama with a fish in her mouth! Snowball and Icicle jumped with joy and said, "Next time we will catch our own fish."

17   Oliver and the Cardinal

Oliver the cat ate only birds. He often hid behind bushes and waited for a bird to fall down from the trees. Then he pounced on it and gobbled it up. One day, on seeing a cardinal near the tree, Oliver attacked him. However, the bird flew off and jeered at Oliver, "You can't catch me!" Angry Oliver stomped back into the bush, but he never gave up so easily. He kept a close vigil on the cardinal who was now preparing his nest for an afternoon nap. When the bird was fast asleep, Oliver quietly climbed the tree. Just as he reached the branch where the cardinal was sleeping, he peered to have a look at the bird. "If the bird is so beautiful I wonder how delicious its meat will be!" thought Oliver. His mouth watered at the thought. He quietly crept forward on the branch. Just as he reached the nest, his paw slipped. Somehow managing to grab the branch, Oliver hung from it. Meanwhile, the cardinal woke up and discovered the cat hanging helplessly. "Now it's my turn, you evil cat," said the cardinal and pecked on Oliver's paws. "Ouch!" cried Oliver. He swore never to eat a bird again and shifted his focus to rats.

18 Tickle Me Silly

One day, a group of mice gathered around a huge chunk of cheese. While they were enjoying their food, their neighbour, Ronald, the wicked cat, arrived. "Oh! This looks like a superb meal," he said, smacking his tongue. However, one mouse saw Ronald approaching and shrieked, "Everybody run!" The mice darted into the haystack. Ronald was heartbroken. As he turned to go, he noticed a tiny tail wriggling inside the block of cheese. It was Malcolm, the silly mouse who was still enjoying his cheese. Seeing Ronald moving closer, the other mice were worried about Malcolm. They darted towards Ronald and crawled all over him. Some tickled his paws, others played with his tail, while some pulled his whiskers. Ronald ran away and swore never to return.

19 The Rainbow Bear

Isis the bear, was very unhappy and dejected with the colour of her fur. "I am all white, while all my friends are so colourful and beautiful," she thought. Indeed, Isis was dull and boring and colourless compared to her friends. Peter the peacock had red, blue and golden feathers, Zack the zebra had black and white stripes and Polly the parrot had a bright green body with a red beak. Isis was very upset and sat wondering what to

do. Right then, the clouds thundered and the rains came pouring down. After a while, the sun shone and a colourful rainbow decorated the sky. Isis decided, "I will fly through the rainbow and colour my fur." She floated through the rainbow and emerged with its vibrant colours on her fur. Henceforth, Isis never again had a gloomy face and did not compare himself to the other animals.

20 The Kites and the Swans

In olden times, kites and swans were blessed with an amazing talent. They could sing very well and used to entertain everyone with their melodious voice. They would even sing in the king's court. One day, they heard the neigh of a horse. They were delighted and wished that they could also neigh. So, they tried very hard to imitate that sound. As a result, they forgot what they knew best—to sing. No one came to hear them anymore and praise their beautiful songs. In the desire to learn something that was not fit for them, they lost what they already had. This little story carries a message. We should be happy with what we have rather than desiring what others possess.

21 The Trouts' Journey

Two trouts, Olive and Brooke, were bored of swimming in the mountain spring. So, they set off downstream. On the way they were caught in a pool of rapids. Brooke and Olive were used to only the calm waters of the spring. The unruly rapids hurled them high into the air. However, they soon controlled their fins and tails and were back in the water, "Oh, what a bumpy ride it is!" cried out Olive. As the fast current carried them away, Brooke felt the warm sunshine on his scales. He noticed some green rocks on the way. "Look at those rocks, they are covered with moss!" he called out to Olive. Suddenly, Olive exclaimed, "Your scales are shining!" "That's the sunshine on my silver scales!" explained Brooke. They noticed many flowers along the banks of the river. There were colourful butterflies fluttering and among them was a grasshopper, quietly poised on a plant. The fish shared a glance that said the grasshopper would make a tasty meal. After lunch, they resumed their journey and came to a spot where they noticed children playing on the banks. The children squealed when they saw the attractive trouts. Seeing a huge net being hurled towards them, Brooke and Olive leaped across and escaped. They were completely taken aback by this unfortunate incident. Soon they saw a school of fish and knew that they were at their destination. It was the beginning of an exciting future for Brooke and Olive.

22 The Greedy Fox

One day, Frizzy Fox and Harry Hare saw a woman carrying a basket of freshly baked cakes and hatched a plan to steal them. Harry told Frizzy that he would feign sickness in front of the woman and when she kept her basket aside to attend to him, Frizzy should run away with it so that later both of them could enjoy the cakes together.

Everything went per plan and Frizzy ran away with the basket. However, he was too hungry to wait and gulped down the entire cake. When Harry arrived, he was very annoyed with Frizzy and decided to take revenge. The intelligent hare asked Frizzy to dip his tail in the water to attract fish. Frizzy did as he was told, not realising that the icy water would freeze his tail. After sometime he pulled his tail, but it snapped. The hare jeered at the greedy fox.

23 The Old Lion

There was an old and frail lion that lay near his cave. All the other animals, on seeing the king of the jungle in such as state, took advantage of him. One day, the ass came and kicked the lion. The next day, a bull jabbed his horns into his stomach. Finally, a boar rushed towards the dying animal and gave him a heavy blow with his tusks.

The lion lay battered and bruised. He looked up towards the sky and cried out, "Oh Lord! All these puny animals are taking advantage of my frailty. But is it not a disgrace to nature that an animal like me should be treated this way?"

The lion failed to understand that he had once used his strength to torture the weak. These very same animals were now taking their revenge on his inability to fight back.

24 Interdependence

One day, the trees in a forest were having a heated discussion. "These animals come to rest in our shade and dirty the place," said the fir tree. "We must teach these animals a lesson," cried the sal tree. "Calm down, my friends. Getting rid of these animals can harm us instead," explained the old banyan tree. He continued, "We trees, animals and men are all interdependent and cannot do without each other." The other trees refused to listen to him. One day, when the animals arrived they swayed so violently that the animals fled in terror. The trees were now happy that no animals visited them. One day, two woodcutters arrived with their axes. The trees heard them talking among themselves, "Finally, these animals have stopped coming here. Now we can peacefully cut the trees for wood." Saying this, they chopped the sal tree while the others watched helplessly.

25 The Flies and the Honey Pot

One day, a jar of honey broke in a kitchen. Some flies, which lived there, at once swarmed towards it and started relishing the honey. So absorbed were they eating honey that they did not even notice that their wings and feet were getting smeared with the sticky honey.

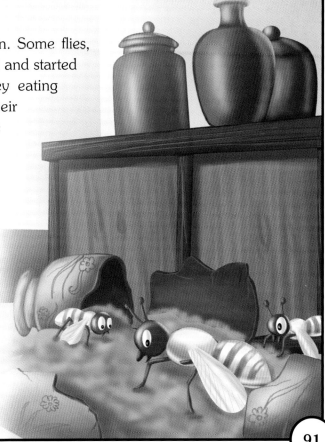

Having feasted to their heart's content, it was now time for them to leave. They tried to flap their wings, but they could not move. Then they tried to lift their feet but that too remained fixed to the table. Anxiously one fly cried, "Oh! Our greed has led us to our doom. We were so blinded by our hunger that we did not see the honey sticking to our bodies."

Just then, a man entered to clean the kitchen. He took out a fly swatter and killed all of them. So wise men say, "Greed is a sin and brings your downfall!"

26 Lily Learns a Lesson

It was winter again and like always, all the butterflies flew to warmer locations in the south. But Lily did not want to do so. When all the butterflies flew south, Lily decided not to follow them. Instead, she slipped away and fluttered towards the north.

She crossed icy lakes, frosty trees and snow-capped mountains. It was such a beautiful sight. She wondered why the other butterflies never ventured to the north. "I am glad I didn't go with them," she thought, "this is so much better. Look at the mountains. I have never seen anything as pretty as this before."

As she soared higher and higher, she noticed a dense cloud and heard a great buzzing sound. "But there are no birds or bees here," she wondered. Suddenly, she saw a huge aeroplane on her right and in a second there was one more approaching from her left. She tried to move further up when another one zoomed down, nearly squashing her.

Soon, the sky was filled with aeroplanes of all shapes and sizes. Just then a pilot shouted, "What are you doing all alone up here when you should be going south?" Lily learnt her lesson and quickly flew down south.

27   The Barn Animals

One day, two pigs and two ducks left their farm and went to play in the nearby pond. "It's so dirty in the barn, at least we can clean ourselves with the water here," said Phil the pig. "And there's fish to eat instead of tasteless apples and pears," cried Dina the duck. They swam, splashed wa-ter, and enjoyed themselves. As it started to darken, they grew anxious. "Let's all walk back close together," said Perry, the second pig. Suddenly, they saw a huge shadow in front of them. Everyone ran helter-skelter, thinking it was a monster. Just then, the moon came out and they realised it was their farmer. "Don't you know that there are wild animals in there who could eat you up?" he said angrily. They agreed it was safer to stay in the dirty barn than be eaten by wild animals.

28   The Peasant and the Eagle

Once, there lived a kind peasant. One day, coming back home from the woods, he spotted an eagle. The bird was caught in a hunter's trap. The kind-hearted peasant set the bird free. The eagle was very grateful to the peasant and vowed to repay his kindness. Another day, the eagle was flying in the sky when he saw the kind peasant sitting under a crumbling wall to eat his lunch. Aware of the danger, the eagle swooped low and flew away with the peasant's lunch. Angrily, the man chased the bird for some distance before it dropped his lunch gently on the ground. When the peasant came back to the old wall, he found that it had crumbled down. What would have happened if he were sitting there at that time! Now, the peasant realised this was the same eagle who was returning his kind deed by saving his life.

29 Creatures of the Sea

Shauna the bright yellow starfish lived in the shallow sea. She had five arms protruding from the centre. Shauna loved living in the sea. Her friend Ally the sea urchin, who had sharp spikes, also loved the shallow seas. However, Kylie the grumpy crab, hated the shallow sea. His constant efforts at jumping into the deep sea from the rocks always failed. Each time he failed, his mood became gloomier. Shauna and Ally tried to cheer him up, "Come on, Kylie, the shallow sea has its own beauty and delights. The big fish and sharks may gobble you up in the deep sea." However, Kylie refused to cheer up. One day, a rowdy group of children who had come to the sea, playfully threw some sand at them. Kylie quickly covered her eyes with her claws while Ally closed her mouth tightly. Shauna anxiously swam across to see if any one was hurt. Kylie angrily said, "Now you see why I hate living in the shallow sea? Anybody can harm us, especially pesky kids." Right then a gigantic tidal wave washed over them and everybody lost their hold and were thrown helter-skelter. It is said the sea brings back whatever it takes. The sea soon brought them back into the shallow waters. Shauna and Ally were overjoyed to return to their old dwelling, while Kylie still grumbled.

30 The Silly Cats

Once there were three silly cats, Smoky, Dusty and Rocky. One day, they decided to catch some birds. But they were too scared to climb the high trees. So they decided to climb a smaller tree. As they climbed the tree, they found that the branches were too weak to carry their weight. Dusty said, "No wonder birds make their nests on such high trees. It's safer up there." The cats were hungry after climbing the tree. Smoky had an idea, "Why not go and catch fish?" The three went to the river and caught a variety of fish. While they sat below a tree and relished their food, they heard the chirping of birds. Rocky looked up wistfully and said, "Maybe better luck next time." Cats, till this day, live with the handicap of being unable to climb trees!

31 The Clumsy Lizard

Logan was a large lizard who lived in a dark cave. Every morning he followed a particular route to find his food. One morning, as he sped through the woods, he saw some white daisies. The flowers were so beautiful that he did not notice Vanora the sheep ahead of him. He bumped into Vanora who jumped in fright and fell with a thud. He yelled angrily at Logan, "You clumsy lizard!" Logan said sorry and ran to the riverbank.

Some plants and creepers grew on the banks of the river. A long brown vine caught Logan's attention and he pulled it with great strength. "Yikes!" shrieked Molly the donkey. "Can't you see that it's my tail?" she shouted. She kicked him so hard that the poor reptile went flying and landed on Irving the wild cat's tail. Irving's tail immediately bent and remained so forever. Irving snarled at Molly, while two pigeons, who saw the incident, called Logan names and asked him to keep away from them. While walking back with a lowered head, Logan brushed against the plants so hard that all the grasshoppers that clung to them fell down. They too shouted at Logan, calling him names. Logan locked himself in his cave and did not come out for several days. As tears rolled down his cheeks he thought, "Why am I so clumsy?" However, soon the animals started missing Logan. They apologised for being rude to him and warmly welcomed him back to the woods.

Contents

The Story of the Month: The Lion and the Jackal

The Story of the Month

The Lion and the Jackal

01 The Lion and the Jackal

The rains lashed the jungle for many days. The lion, the king of the jungle, thought of a brilliant plan. He called his army of a baboon, a tortoise, a hyena, a jackal and some monkeys. "Friends," he said, "let us build a dam to store all the rainwater for the dry season."

The animals worked day and night to build the dam—all except the wicked jackal. Once the dam was complete, he was, however, the first one to drink water from it. The monkeys complained to their king. "Guard the dam carefully!" ordered the lion handing a long stick to the baboon. When the jackal found the baboon guarding the dam, he quickly thought of a plan to trick the baboon. He knew that the baboon loved honey, so he got a jar and said aloud, "What do I care for that water in the dam? I have sweet honey in this jar." The baboon's mouth watered and he asked the jackal for a few drops of honey. "I'll give you some but first you must let me tie you up," said the wily jackal. The foolish baboon agreed. The jackal quickly tied him tightly with a rope and laughed, "You are a good-for-nothing guard!"

When the lion heard this, he was furious. He called an emergency meeting. Everyone thought hard how to teach the jackal a lesson. At last, his minister, the tortoise, came up with a plan. He asked the hyena to place a huge stone near the dam and cover it well with glue. When the jackal saw the stone, he thought, "Oh, the animals have placed a stepping-stone to help me reach the water." But lo! As soon as he stepped on it he was stuck! Just then the tortoise crept from behind a boulder

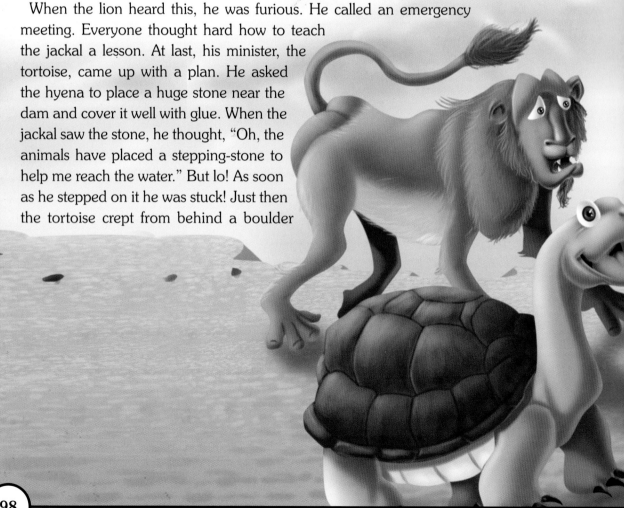

and jeered at the jackal. The jackal pleaded to be set free, but the tortoise was unmoved. "No way, your punishment is death. Tell us your last wish," he declared. The cunning jackal replied, "I want you to shave my tail and rub it with fat." The tortoise asked the hyena to free the jackal so that his tail could be shaved. Once the jackal was set free, he jumped up and sped away. Everybody including the lion followed him. They chased him off to the edge of the cliff. The jackal grabbed the edge of the cliff and screamed for help. Seeing his plight, the lion decided to help. The wise tortoise said, "O' Mighty King! Don't help an ungrateful animal like the jackal." "I promise to mend my ways. Please save me," begged the jackal. The generous lion climbed down carefully and extended his hand to the jackal. The ungrateful animal crawled out safely and pushed the lion into the grave ditch. All the other furious animals chased the jackal out of the jungle never to be seen again.

02 The Buffalo, the Field Mouse and the Fox

One day while gathering wild beans, a field mouse saw a hungry buffalo chewing away all the grass. He immediately asked the buffalo to leave. When the harmless buffalo refused, the mouse hopped onto him and bit his ears. Unable to bear the pain, the buffalo fell unconscious. A fox, which happened to pass by, saw the mouse and the unconscious buffalo. He smacked his lips and thought, "There's not only a dead buffalo but also a mouse to eat!" He quickly approached the mouse and kindly asked if he could eat the buffalo. The mouse readily agreed. "But my wife will be hungry too. I will need some more meat," said the greedy fox. "Where do I get more meat for you?" asked the mouse. "I can eat you!" said the fox and he pounced on the mouse.

03 The Stag at the Pool

One day, while drinking water from a lake, a stag saw his own reflection in the water. He saw his long and wavy horns and greatly admired it. Then he saw his legs and wondered why they looked so lean and weak. While the disappointed stag pondered on his legs, a lion appeared before him. Seeing the stag, the lion waited to pounce on it. The stag ran as fast as he could and went inside a wood. However, his long horns got entangled in a wild creeper and he tried hard to free them. The lion followed right behind and attacked the stag. In his dying moments the stag thought, "I despised that which could have saved me and glorified the one which brought about my destruction."

04   The Fighting Cocks and the Eagle

One day, a farmer found two chicks on his doorstep. "Cheep! Cheep! We are lost," wept one. The kind farmer took them inside. He made a wooden coop for them and fed them with grains. He named the chicks Coodle and Doodle. They kept fighting with each other over food. One day, after a big fight, Coodle went and hid in the granary. "I am the master of this coop. Coodle belongs to the granary!" Doodle crowed loudly. An eagle flying overhead heard him. He swooped down and gobbled him up. The eagle hid near the door waiting for Coodle. When Coodle came out of the granary, the eagle pounced on him and carried him to his eyrie. "How foolish we were to quarrel amongst ourselves. I have now become a meal for the eagle family," thought Coodle unhappily.

05   The Monkey and the Wedge

Once, a wealthy merchant decided to build a temple. He employed lots of masons and carpenters to construct the temple. The area was full of blocks of marbles and logs of wood. The carpenters and masons would start work in the morning and break for lunch at noon. One day, when the carpenters and masons were away for lunch, some monkeys came to the site. They were having a lovely time playing with the marbles and logs. Suddenly, one of the monkeys saw a partly sawed log with a wedge in the middle. Curious, he sat on the log and scratched his head wondering what to do next. He started tugging at the wedge violently. Finally, the wedge came off but alas! One of the monkeys' leg got trapped in the rift. He howled in pain. The carpenters came to see what was happening and helped the monkey free his leg. All the monkeys ran away and promised to stay out of mischief thereafter.

06 Stanley Bear Makes Friends

It was a bright morning. Stanley the bear went to the woods in search of food. "Ooo-la-la, spring is here!" sang Stanley. A beaver, a raccoon, some birds and a few butterflies who were enjoying the sunshine heard him. Seeing the big bear, the animals were scared. "Run!" shouted the raccoon. Stanley was hurt to hear the animals accuse him in this way. He said, "Don't run away from me. I am your friend!" "He is tricking us," said the beaver. "Don't believe him!" chirped the birds. Unable to convince them, the lonely bear went to a nearby tree. Seeing a cater-pillar, he said, "Oh! what an unfortunate animal I am. I have no friends. Everybody thinks I eat up animals when the truth is I only eat berries, fish and honey." The butterfly, who had followed the bear, overheard him. He immediately flew to his other friends and told them the truth about the bear. All the animals apologised. Stanley was happy once again as they all became his friends.

07 Food Fight

Aileen, Betty, Shannon and Matilda were bird chicks who lived together. One morning, Aileen went to pluck some figs. Unfortunately her claw slipped and all the figs fell. "Ouch!" screamed someone. She peered from behind a branch and saw Betty. Betty's head was covered with the fig pulp and she looked very angry. Aileen flew away to hide in an old castle nearby. Betty looked around and saw Shannon on another tree. "She must have thrown those figs," thought Betty. She picked up the rest of the figs and hurled them at Shannon covering her with the sticky pulp. "Who did that?" Shannon screamed angrily. Betty quickly flew away to the old castle. Wiping off the pulp, Shannon collected some figs and went in search of the culprit. She found Matilda digging the ground. "I am sure she's looking for a place to hide," thought Shannon and threw the figs at her. Before Matilda could scream for help, Shannon flew away to the old castle. Meanwhile, Matilda gathered some figs and chased after her. She found Aileen hiding behind a stone and threw the figs at her. Before long, figs were flying everywhere. Soon, all the friends were having a great time. Alas! Mama Bird flew in and scolded all for playing with their food. She shooed them all out of the castle.

08 The Elephant and the Mice

Borko the elephant bullied all the other animals in the jungle. He would ask them to get his food, massage his legs and gather logs and if they refused, he would crush them with his mighty feet. To get rid of him, all the animals called a meeting. The dog said, "I know elephants are scared of mice." "How can a huge elephant be scared of a tiny mouse?" asked the lion. The dog explained, "If all the mice hop over Borko and tease him, he will run away." All the animals were impressed with the idea and the mice were assigned the great task. Next when Borko came to bully the animals, the mice jumped on him. Some pulled his ears, some his tail, while others poked his eyes. Borko was scared and ran away from the jungle. All the other animals lived happily ever after.

09 The Feather Pillow

Andrew the mouse lay in his hole tossing and turning. "This pillow is old and too soft, I need a new one," he cried and walked out of the hole. Three birds perched on a tree branch were merrily twittering. Andrew looked up at the birds and thought, "Birds have feathers and I can use these to make a feather pillow." An idea struck him and he decided to scare them so that they might shake off their feathers. So he quietly went behind the tree and climbed it. Perching himself on a higher branch, he let out such a loud shriek that the birds were scared. They started flapping their wings vigorously and their feathers scattered around the tree like rain. Andrew scurried down and began collecting the feathers. That night, he made a feather pillow and slept peacefully.

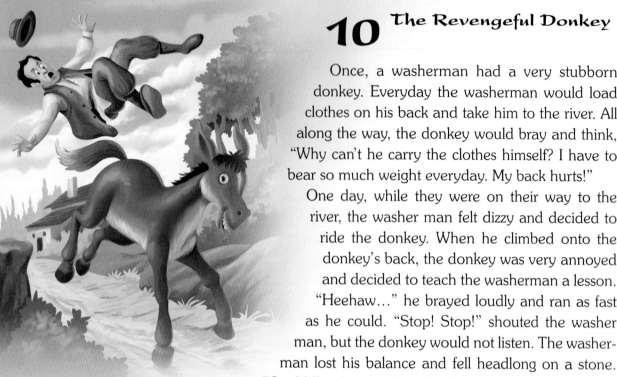

10 The Revengeful Donkey

Once, a washerman had a very stubborn donkey. Everyday the washerman would load clothes on his back and take him to the river. All along the way, the donkey would bray and think, "Why can't he carry the clothes himself? I have to bear so much weight everyday. My back hurts!"

One day, while they were on their way to the river, the washer man felt dizzy and decided to ride the donkey. When he climbed onto the donkey's back, the donkey was very annoyed and decided to teach the washerman a lesson. "Heehaw…" he brayed loudly and ran as fast as he could. "Stop! Stop!" shouted the washer man, but the donkey would not listen. The washerman lost his balance and fell headlong on a stone. "Ouch! I've fractured my leg," moaned the washerman in pain while the donkey ran away.

11 A New Spring Day

The soft rays of the sun caressed the earth. "Wake up! It's a new day," it seemed to say. The tulips and daffodils opened their petals to welcome the day. The leaves shone brightly and birds and bees flocked the trees. Ben the baby bunny, went to the fields to play with his friends, the ducklings, the bluebird and robin and the pony. Ben ate his carrot while the others nibbled the seeds and apples. Bruno the bear woke up from his long sleep and brought his family out in the sun. Matilda the butterfly flew merrily from flower to flower. The sunlight falling on the running stream made the water sparkle like a thousand stars. All the animals frolicked and shouted and played with each other. All the sounds seem to say, "Welcome Spring!"

12 The Lost Mouse

When Baby Mouse fell asleep, Mama Mouse went out of the hole in search of food. Meanwhile, Baby Mouse woke up and unable to find his mama, he hopped out of the hole to find her. Suddenly, he noticed a huge field filled with flowers. He forgot about his mama and went into the field. He peered inside a flower and found a bumblebee. The bumblebee jumped on his nose and stung him bitterly. He was so scared that he ran through the flowers, but after a while he realised that he had lost his way. Now he was even more scared and started to cry. Then he heard a voice, "Where are you, Baby Mouse?" It was his mother! Baby Mouse ran in the direction of the voice and saw his mother. She hugged him and warned him not to go out of the hole till he grew up.

13 Beans the Greedy Cat

Beans was a very greedy cat. Everyday his owner gave him some fish and milk, but Beans still remained hungry. He would go to the garden to look for worms, butterflies or birds. All the crows in the neighbourhood knew what a greedy cat Beans was and flew away when Beans came to the garden. One day, Beans saw a bright green grasshopper and pounced on it. But no sooner had he begun eating it, the other grasshoppers in the garden came to rescue their friend from the clutches of the cat. Some nibbled his ears, some bit his tail, while the others poked his nose. "Meow!" cried Beans. The crows came rushing to the garden and saw Beans trying his best to escape from the swarm of grasshoppers. They swooped down and caught the grasshoppers in their beaks. Later, Beans thanked the crows and promised never to be greedy again!

14 How Bunny Stole the Elephant's Dinner

One fine day, while roaming in the forest, Bunny, the rabbit saw Polo the Elephant busy cooking dinner. "Beans for dinner! I am sure they'll be delicious!" thought Bunny smacking his lips. When Polo was fast asleep, Bunny quietly crept into the kitchen and ate all the beans. Next morning, when Polo discovered the empty bowl, he was furious and asked a lion to guard his house. Now Bunny overheard Polo's plan and laid a trap near the elephant's house. Next day, he ate the elephant's dinner and was about to leave when the lion pounced on him. But alas! The lion's leg was caught in the trap. Polo decided to go to Tambo, the wise tortoise of the forest for help. "Smear me with salt and put me into your dinner tomorrow and I will catch the thief," assured Tambo. The next day as soon as Bunny put his mouth into the bowl, Tambo popped his head out and bit the rabbit's nose. When Bunny was being taken to the prison, Polo said to him, "Bunny, you should work for your food and not steal somebody else's."

15 The Silly Raven

One day, a raven flew to a yard where the peacocks used to play. Some beautiful feathers of the peacocks were lying scattered on the ground. The raven collected a few feathers and tied them to his tail. He then flew away. The peacocks that were returning from the forest saw the raven and were angry at what he had done. "Such a silly bird that raven is," they said. "By sticking our feathers he thinks he can be one of us!" declared one peacock. "Let us teach him a lesson," suggested another. They pecked at him and bullied him. The raven flew away to join his own clan. He met the other birds who laughed and made fun of him. When he reached his clan, the other ravens were also very annoyed with him. They said to him, "You should be ashamed of yourself. You have disgraced our clan. As a punishment, from today you will not stay with us."

16 The Big Pumpkin

Jiggles the rat used to wait anxiously for the big orange pumpkins to grow in the fields every year. He would climb on top of them and declare them his own. He never shared the pumpkins. This year, however, the pumpkins were taking far too long to turn orange. Jiggles was worried that someone might attack his pumpkin, so he starved for days and guarded it. However, one day he couldn't bear his hunger any longer. Seeing a crow flying overhead, he called out for help. The crow agreed to guard the pumpkin while Jiggles went in search of food. The moment Jiggles left, the crow whistled to his friends and within minutes they ate the pumpkin. When Jiggles saw the condition of his pumpkin, he screamed at the crow. The crow mocked at Jiggles, saying, "This is what happens to a greedy rat." Henceforth, Jiggles shared his pumpkins with the other rats.

17 Chirrup the Donkey

Chirrup was no ordinary donkey. He could run really fast, often as fast as the Cheetah, but he was also gifted with the most terrible voice. When he brayed, all the animals ran away. Now Chirrup wanted to marry Nolly, the most beautiful donkey in the jungle. Nolly agreed on the condition that Chirrup should become king of the jungle. So Chirrup went to the lion and expressed his desire to become the king. The lion snarled and chased him away. Chirrup was quite upset. "If I don't become the king, Nolly will not marry me!" he wailed. Then an idea dawned on him. Early morning, he went to the lion's den and began braying. The lion covered his ears but Chirrup brayed so loudly that the lion could still hear him. Finally, the lion offered Chirrup the post of the king and Nolly happily married him.

18 Oranges and Lemons

Jiggles and Farmy were two rabbits. Jiggles lived in an orange orchard while Farmy lived in a lemon orchard. One day, when Jiggles went to his orchard he saw Farmy nibbling at the oranges. "How dare you touch my oranges?" asked Jiggles. "The orange fell on my side of the fence," clarified Farmy. Jiggles went to the lemon orchard and plucked a few lemons. Now Farmy was furious. He scurried up Jiggles' orange tree and began throwing the oranges. There was a shower of oranges and lemons. Finally, the two rabbits grew tired. They quickly collected the fruits and went home. At night Jiggles kept staring at the lemons wandering what to do. Farmy stared at the oranges and didn't know what to do either." Suddenly an idea struck him. He made orange juice. While he was busy making the juice, he heard a knock. On opening the door he saw Jiggles. "I have made lemonade, will you have some?" asked Jiggles. The two rabbits realised their mistake and agreed to work together.

19 Worm Giggles

Wylie the worm never smiled. One day, his friends decided to make Wylie laugh. Wendy crawled on a tree branch and pranced all over. Wylie saw her but did not laugh. Willie collected the tiny bugs and juggled them, still Wylie's face remained stern. All the worms came and performed their tricks. Some danced, some sang, some mimicked, but a smile did not appear on Wylie's mouth. Finally, Walter, a young worm crept out of the crowd. "I have a plan!" he said excitedly. He quickly gathered cans of paint and coloured all the worms. Then he took his brush and started colouring Wylie. Everybody was scared that Wylie might scream back at Walter. But lo! Wylie laughed as the soft brush touched his body. Since then, Wylie always wore a smile on his lips.

20   I Caught a Fish This Big

On a bright spring morning, Edward the bear ran down to the river. He was going to fish all by himself. As Edward waddled through the water, he saw different coloured fishes leaping about. Seeing a green fish, he dived forward, but the fish had already jumped back into the water. He tried for long but couldn't catch any fish. Just when all his hopes were dashed, he saw a big pink fish taking a great leap. Edward ran and grabbed the fish before it could slip into the water. The fish wriggled in his mouth and was about to escape. Edward caught it with his paw and held on tightly. "I have succeeded," he exclaimed. He ran home to tell his mother. "Edward, you have grown up. You caught your first fish!" his mother congratulated him. She cooked the fish in Edward's favourite way.

21   Where Is Everybody?

One fine morning, when Pablo the donkey woke up from his sleep, he saw his house empty. "Where are Mama and Papa?" he wondered. He went out and saw that the streets were deserted too. None of his friends or neighbours were around. Pablo became sad because it was his birthday today. "I thought everybody was going to throw a big party for me," he mumbled. He walked down to his favourite shop, Senor Pecos' Pizza shop. However, Senor Pecos wasn't there either. Almost on the verge of tears now, Pablo wept, "Even Senor Pecos did not remember my birthday!" Pablo decided to go to the town square where he was sure to come across some known person, but not a single soul was there. Pablo sat down and started to cry. Suddenly, "Happy Birthday, Pablo!" cried out a number of voices. Pablo stood startled. Mama, Papa and the people of the town were standing there with a cake. "You remembered! Thank you, everyone," said Pablo. That day everybody celebrated Pablo's birthday with great joy.

22 Easter Eggs

Peter the bunny loved distributing chocolate eggs on Easter. He decorated each egg with great care. In the evening, all his friends—the rabbit, the cat, the giraffe came to greet Peter and collect the eggs. They all relished the chocolate eggs and thanked Peter for it. However, Peter felt sad that nobody got any gift for him. Suddenly, all his friends cried out "Happy Easter, Peter!" Peter was surprised to find his friends holding a huge chocolate egg decorated with ribbons. "Every year you gift us chocolate eggs. We thought we should also do something nice for you," cried his friends. Peter thanked his friends. This was his best Easter ever.

23 Four Baby Birds

Betty, Billy, Bobby and Bonnie were four baby birds. One day, their mother said, "Today all of you will fly down and bring a worm each." Betty, Billy and Bobby were very excited. They were eagerly looking forward to the day when they could flap their wings and soar high above. However, Bonnie was scared. "What if I forget to flap my wings?" she wondered. One by one, she saw all her siblings taking the plunge. Betty and Billy went first. They threw open their wings and flew away. Bobby just dropped down, but in a second was floating in the air. It was Bonnie's turn now and her mother said, "If you do not fly, you cannot get food for yourself." Now there was no way out, she had to go. Anxiously, Bonnie came to the edge of the branch and closing her eyes, finally took the plunge. Her wings swung open and she soared higher and higher. "Hey, I can fly too!" she screamed.

24 Coyote Brings Fire

One day, the animals in the wild decided to get fire from the fire beings, who guarded it. An old coyote led the group of animals. The animals hid behind a bush and the coyote walked to the bonfire. "Who's that?" asked a fire being. "That's an old coyote," replied another. The coyote quietly lay down. Right then, the animals began a terrible noise—some howled while others yelled. The worried fire beings went to investigate. The coyote was waiting for this. He grabbed a piece of burning wood and slipped away. However, one of the fire beings saw him and ran behind. Unable to keep pace with the coyote, he flung a smoldering wood towards the coyote, which burnt the tip of his tail. The coyote quickly threw the fire at the squirrel, who caught it in his tail and ran. The fire scorched the squirrel's tail and curled it up. The chipmunk came to the squirrel's rescue and ran with the fire. However, one of the fire beings clawed the chipmunk's back leaving three stripes on it. The chipmunk hurled the fire at the frog, who leaped at great speed. The fire beings caught hold of the frog's tail and pulled it so hard that it snapped. But the agile frog slipped out of their hands and ran away with the fire. The animals got the fire but in the process left the coyote with a white tail, the squirrel with a curly tail, the chipmunk with a striped back and the frog without a tail.

25 The Bakery Bear

One day, while Brenda was baking cakes in her bakery, she saw a brown bear climbing through the window. Grabbing a broomstick, she tried to scare the animal away, but it growled so loud that Brenda ran away. She quickly called Bill, the policeman, who arrived with a huge net. The bear charged at Bill and chased him away. Meanwhile, Brenda called Barney, the local dog catcher. Barney arrived in a blue van. He asked Brenda to go back into the kitchen and prepare some delicious honey and butter biscuits. Once the biscuits were made, Barney opened the door of his van and started stocking the biscuits. Sniffing the sweet scent of biscuits, the bear quickly jumped onto the van. Then Barney closed the door and drove away to the jungle, where he let the bear out.

26 The Boar and the Man

Once a fox and a wild boar were talking. The fox said, "Man is much stronger than us." But the boar did not agree and said, "I can prove you wrong." So they decided that the boar would have a duel with a man to prove who is stronger.

The next day, the fox showed the boar a hunter with a gun and sword. The boar at once jumped on the hunter, but the hunter fired back. The boastful boar made all attempts to fight the man. Then the hunter fired another shot at the boar. The boar grunted and tried to grab the hunter from below. This time, the hunter stabbed the boar with his sword. The wounded boar returned to the fox, in great pain. The fox said, "You boasted too much and because of that you are suffering."

27 Beehive Surprise

Little Colin the baby bear, watched closely as bees swarmed around a beehive. "What's that on the tree?" he asked his mother. "That's a beehive," replied Mama Bear. "Bears love honey and that's where you get honey from," she explained. After sometime, Mama Bear returned with a stick. "What's that stick for?" enquired Colin. "You need to knock down their home to extract honey," said Mama. Colin looked up at the beehive and wondered what would happen to the bees if they stroke their hive with the stick. "I cannot destroy their home," cried out Colin. His mother was surprised. Even the cautious bees were startled. "They are not harming us, so why should I harm them?" explained Colin. His mother was angry with Colin and left immediately. The bees were so thankful to Colin that they supplied him with lots of honey every day.

28 Wheat

Marti and Mimsi, the two wild rats, used to eat all the wheat in Farmer Jo's field. One day, farmer Jo had a bright idea. He went to the market and looked for a cat. He saw many cats, but he wanted a special one. At last, he found a cat whose complexion matched the colour of the wheat. "Ah," thought the farmer, "now I have a mean to catch those rats!" He named the cat Wheat. At night, he asked Wheat to hide in the field and wait for the rats. That night, the rats arrived as usual. They could not see Wheat hiding among the wheat ears. When the rats neared, Wheat pounced on them and killed them. Farmer Jo was very happy with Wheat. He fed him well and Wheat in turn made sure that no rat ever entered the field.

29 A Pole and Some Worms

One day when Gilbert, the brown bear, went fishing he saw that he had a pole but no worms to attract the fish. While pondering over the problem, he saw his friend Sidney approaching the river. "Why are you looking so sad?" asked Sidney. When Gilbert explained his problem, Sidney cried, "And I have forgotten the pole." While the two sat wondering what to do, the fish hopped and leapt about. Suddenly an idea dawned on Sidney. "Since I have the worms and you the pole, why not share and take turns to fish?" Gilbert's eyes lit up. That morning, the two friends fished to their heart's content. While heading home, they thanked each other for the help and went home to savour delicious fried fish.

30 Miko the Monkey

Miko the monkey had six brothers but none loved him. One day, it rained so hard that the entire forest was flooded. Miko and his brothers had to stay on the high branches of the trees for several days, without any food. Soon, they became weak and started falling sick. "I must do something to help my brothers!" thought Miko. Just then, he saw a banana tree but it was too far for him to jump. But brave Miko took one huge leap and landed on the banana tree. He plucked a few bananas and leaped back to his tree. He gave the bananas to his brothers and went back to get some more. His brothers thanked him for saving their life. Miko was very happy. His brothers apologised for being mean to him and hugged him.

Contents

The Story of the Month

Safety in Numbers

01 Safety in Numbers

Feeya the fly was flying around looking for other flies as she always felt safe in a crowd. She looked all around and saw a melon lying on the ground. "Bhooo…" Feeya flew and settled herself on the melon. "Yum…It smells sweet and tasty," thought Feeya, licking her lips. Spooky, the spider hanging on a wall nearby watched Feeya and decided to have her for a meal. When Feeya was relishing the sweet melon, Spooky called out,

"Will you walk into my parlour?
To be friendly, Dear Feeya
Do come in and spare some time
And let the bells of friendship chime"

Feeya looked up and saw Spooky hanging in his cobweb. She could make out that the grin in Spooky's face was not a friendly gesture and refused saying,

"Nay, nay Spooky, my dear
I can sense danger very near
You intend to feed on me
So it's neither friendship nor tea"

And so, Feeya darted away to the nearby mango tree. She looked around desperately for the other flies but could see none in sight. "I wonder where all of them have gone," thought Feeya in dismay. Suddenly she remembered the old Jackfruit tree. It was summer and time for the jackfruits to be ripe and delicious. All the flies went to feed on the jackfruits. "Ptshhh…Oh, I am sure they are having a feast," thought Feeya and flew towards the old Jackfruit tree. On the way Feeya met Buzzy the bee. "Hey Feeya, where are you rushing to?" asked Buzzy. "Oh, I'm on my way to the old Jackfruit tree to meet the other flies," said Feeya in a hurry. "No, no don't go there. All your friends and family have got stuck in a flypaper that was spread on one of its branches," warned Buzzy. "Don't be silly. Why will someone spread flypaper there?" retorted Feeya quite arrogantly. "Let's go together to the Jackfruit tree and check," suggested Feeya and the two of them went towards the tree. When they were a little distance away from the old Jackfruit tree, Buzzy pointed out, "Look! There they are. All glued to the flypaper." Feeya flew a little ahead and said, "Can't you see them flapping their wings and dancing?" "Dancing? They are trying to free themselves from the flypaper. Listen to my advice and avoid going there, else you'll meet with the same fate," said Buzzy and flew away. Longing to be in company with the other flies, Feeya flew onto the branch of the Jackfruit tree where her friends and family were. But alas! Poor Feeya got stuck along with the others. "I should have listened to Buzzy's advice," she wailed, realising her mis-take. But it was too late.

02 Catch the Worm

Chrissie was a very cunning hen. She enjoyed her life in the farm. She would roam about the farm in search of grains and lay one egg every day. One summer morning, when she was pecking at seeds on the ground, she saw a worm. She was about to peck at the worm when it vanished into a hole. Chrissie was angry at having missed the opportunity. She went back to pecking at seeds but kept her eyes on the hole all the time. After some time, the worm made its way up the hole again. Chrissie was just waiting for this chance but missed it again. Now she decided to hide behind the horse's water barrel and wait. When the little worm stuck its head out this time, he was relieved to see that the hen was not there. But alas! As he crawled out, Chrissie jumped on him up and gobbled him. Happily, she went back to her coop and laid an egg.

03 The Frog in the Shallow Well

A frog that lived in a well was bragging to a turtle that lived in the sea. "I'm so happy here. I can jump around as much as I want. The water comes up to my armpits and I splash it around! The other animals that live here, the worms, the crabs and the tadpoles are nothing compared to me. I'm the master here!" Hearing these words, the turtle went to have a look at the well but his feet got stuck in the mud. Realising the frog's ignorance, he told the frog, "You cannot imagine how wide and deep the sea is. It is so mighty and powerful that the waves can swallow even a big animal. The sea never dries up. Living there gives one the greatest happiness." Now the frog realised that he was just a tiny creature and was ashamed of his bragging.

04 The Wolf and the Shepherd

A wolf had been eyeing a flock of sheep for a long time. He thought of a plan to seize them all. Every day he would quietly follow the sheep but he never harmed them. In the beginning, the shepherd did not trust the wolf and guarded his flock carefully. But as time passed, he started trusting the wolf. The shepherd thought that the wolf was like a guardian to his sheep. One day the shepherd had to go to the city for some work. He asked the wolf to take care of his flock while he was away. At last, the wolf got what he had been waiting for! He attacked the sheep and killed most of them. When the shepherd came back, he realised what a big mistake he had made in trusting a wolf to guard his sheep.

05 The Greedy Seagull

There lived a seagull that would play near the sea the whole day. One day, he was very hungry so he looked around for food. Seeing the fishes playing in the sea he decided to try his luck there. After a little while, he managed to catch a big fish and gulped it down hungrily. Alas! The fish was too large and it burst the seagull's gullet bag. The poor sea gull lay down on the shore in pain. He lamented, "I should have never entered the sea." An eagle was flying by and overhearing the seagull, it exclaimed, "Friend, it was your greed that brought you to this state. Why did you enter the sea when you are a bird of the air? You have no one to blame but yourself."

06 Read a Book

Jeremy the mouse did not want to study. "I hate history and science!" he said. "I don't like to read either," he added. Just then, his mother came to him with a piece of cheese. "Do you know where cheese comes from?" she asked him. Jeremy proudly said, "The refrigerator." "No, it comes from Bonnie, the cow," said his mother. Jeremy was confused. He went to ask Bonnie. She told Jeremy that the grass she ate helped her to produce milk. "But how can grass turn into milk?" he asked. "That happens in my stomach," explained Bonnie. Jeremy was amazed to know that butter, cheese and ice cream are made from milk. Bonnie said that goat and camel milk was also used to make cheese. So, now when Jeremy's mother suggested that she would give him some books to read, he agreed! He wanted to learn everything.

07 Fins

Finlay the whale and Reins the sea horse were very excited as they were going for lunch at Fins' new restaurant under the sea. "It's good that we came early, look at the queue," said Finlay pointing at the long queue. Just then three sharks, Stripes, Nails and Coral swam past quickly and broke the queue. Stripes the tiger shark said, "Now we are first in line," and pushed Reins away. Finlay was much bigger than the sharks and opened his mouth to protest. Reins said, "Leave them, let them go first." The three sharks pounded on the door of the restaurant, "Open the door quickly," they said. The other creatures were frightened and leapt aside. "You big bullies!" said Maine the lobster. The wicked sharks gulped him down in no time. Then they went inside the restaurant and ordered the waitress to bring everything. The sharks finished almost all the food. Finlay was very angry and could not tolerate this. He called three other whales to teach the sharks a lesson. The whales blew as hard as they could and the sharks were blown out of the restaurant. "Hurrah! for Finlay and his friends," shouted the animals.

08 The Dancing Peacock

The handsome golden swan was the king of the birds. He had a beautiful daughter. He had granted her a wish that she could choose her own husband. The king invited birds from far and wide for his daughter to choose a suitable husband.

Birds of all kinds attended the gathering. The king's lovely daughter looked at all the suitors and chose an emerald green and blue peacock to be her husband. The other birds congratulated the peacock on his good luck. The peacock was very thrilled and started dancing in excitement. In his excitement, he forgot all manners and modesty. The king was enraged by the peacock's indecency and said, "I will not let my daughter get married to such a proud and shameless creature who doesn't even know how to behave." Now, the princess was married to the king's nephew and the silly peacock flew away in shame.

09 This is Not Our Egg

Once there were two crocodiles, Carla and Corky. They sat next to their nest, waiting anxiously for the six eggs to hatch. "I will teach my babies how to swim," said Carla. "And I will teach them how to find a cool and shady spot on the bank of the river." said Corky.

They did not realise that another egg had come rolling down the hill and got mixed with their eggs. The crocodile eggs hatched and out came six baby crocodiles, five boys and one girl. Carla and Corky cried in joy to see their young ones. "That's my little baby girl!" exclaimed Carla. Suddenly Corky saw the seventh egg and said, "From where did this seventh egg come? Didn't we have only six eggs? This egg looks a little different." Both were very surprised when the seventh egg hatched and out peeped a duckling! Corky took the six young crocodiles for a swim and Carla took the duckling up the hill to return it to the ducks.

10 The Prickly Purple Patch

Ogilvy the beaver was tired and wanted to take a nap. He looked around the riverbank for a comfortable spot and spotted a patch of purple growing near the brown reeds. "That looks soft and pretty," he mumbled and jumped on the purple thistle. Suddenly, he screamed in pain. He saw that there were prickles inside the thistle. He walked back towards the riverbank, crying. He breathed a sigh of relief on reaching the river and disappeared into the water.

11 Beatrice and Charles

Two chubby pigs, Beatrice and Charles, lived in the cabbage garden of Lord and Lady Cuthbert. One afternoon, Charles told Beatrice that their lives were going to end. "Pigs are fetching really good prices in the market. We too will soon be sold," he told Beatrice. Beatrice consoled her companion saying, "Lord and Lady Cuthbert take good care of us. I don't think they'll harm us." To cheer her friend up, Beatrice took Charles to a rose garden. As they wandered through the rows of roses, a beautiful fairy named Mildred appeared. The fairy fluttered her wings and perched herself on a rose. "Why are you looking so sad?" she asked. "Oh, Mildred! We shall soon sizzle on a frying pan," lamented Charles. "Can you help us?" pleaded Beatrice as a tear ran down her cheek. "Of course, I will," assured Mildred. Meanwhile, the Lord and Lady Cuthbert wondered where the two pigs were. "Thomas, look for them in the cabbage garden," ordered Lord Cuthbert. Thomas set out with his sickle. While clearing weeds, he saw something hidden amidst the thick cabbage leaves. Cutting through the weeds, he found stone statues of Charles and Beatrice. "You two pigs have been blessed. At least, you did not end up in the frying pan!" cried Thomas. Mildred had saved the two pigs!

12 The Big Fright

Some frogs lived in a pretty garden pond that had lovely waterlilies. One day, the owner of the pond placed something new in the pond. The frogs hid themselves till the owner had gone. One bold frog then popped out of the water to have a look and was frightened by what he saw and dived down to tell the other frogs that he had seen a horrible looking bird with a wicked beak. An old frog said, "I think it's a heron. We must be careful because herons eat frogs." The bold frog was annoyed on hearing this and decided to frighten the heron. He swam up and moved straight to the heron's back. But instead of feeling warm feathers, he felt cold metal. The frog slid down the bird's back and was thrown back into the pond. He told the other frogs, "That bird is not real. It's made of metal." Soon the other frogs were also leaping and jumping on the metal heron. They had a merry time!

13 The Lazy Fox

In summer, the foxes used to work hard and gather food for the winter. But Jerry was a lazy fox who liked to lie under the shade of the sunflower all day and listen to the birds singing. Kevin Fox saw him and said, "Jerry, soon it will be winter. You better find food and store it." Lori Fox also told him the same thing but Jerry ignored their advice. He was too busy enjoying the sunshine. One day, the sky was filled with dark, grey clouds. It began to rain heavily. Poor Jerry ran to find a place for shelter. He saw the other foxes hiding in a big hollow oak tree but they did not let him join them. The bears also chased him away. Jerry realised his mistake but it was too late. At last the birds agreed to carry him to the south where it was always warm and there was no need to store food.

14 Wrinkled Winner

A goat, an ass and a camel were walking when they found a bundle of hay lying under a tree. The animals were hungry and were eager to lay their hands on it. The goat said, "The oldest among us should take the hay since it is not enough for all of us." The ass declared, "I was there when Nadir Shah captured Delhi in 1739. That makes me 250 years old!" The goat said, "I'm older than you since I lived at the time of Sultan Muhammad Bin Tughlak." Meanwhile, the camel was busy nibbling at the hay. "Hey, what are you doing?" shouted the goat. "Didn't you say that the oldest amongst us could have the hay? My wrinkled skin and knobbly, joints make me the oldest." And saying this he quietly walked away with the hay.

15 Trixie Spider

Trixie Spider could weave the most beautiful webs. They were so pretty that she had won many prizes at web weaving competitions. But that was when Trixie lived in the jungle. Now poor Trixie had to move to the city. There were no trees here. She had to stay inside people's homes. But people don't like cobwebs in their homes and they swept off her creations all the time. Soon, it was spring and Trixie was really worried. This was the time when people cleaned their homes. She went in search of a place to stay. After a long time, she saw an old house where no one lived. She made a huge big web inside. At night, an old witch with a crooked nose and a black hat entered the house. She saw the web and exclaimed, "What a beautiful cobweb! I must let this spider stay here!" Now, Trixie Spider was very happy for she had a place to stay.

16 Try and Try Again

Bruce the bear was trying to get to the top of a tree to get hold of the beehive. "Ah, that honey must be so sweet," he mumbled to himself. He tried to climb with the help of his sharp claws and large paws but each time he would fall down after climbing a little. Bonnie Beaver saw Bruce's plight and came rushing to help his friend. "Bears are very good at climbing trees. So keep trying till you reach the top!" said Bonnie eagerly. Bruce tried climbing the tree again but again fell down after reaching halfway up. Now Ronnie Raccoon and Bonnie Beaver encouraged Bruce not to give up reaching the top of the tree. "Come on, Bruce, you can easily climb the tree." Bruce gathered courage and again made his way up the tall tree. And to his great joy, Bruce succeeded in reaching the beehive!

17 An Annoying Habit

Gavin was a beautiful grouse who always bragged about himself, "Look at me," he announced whenever he saw any other animal. One day while returning to his nest, he saw a large bird, which had blue and green feathers. There was an exotic design on his feathers and a tuft of beautiful feathers on his forehead, which resembled a crown. He saw Gavin looking at him and said, "It seems you've never seen a beautiful animal like me. I am a peacock." Gavin was indeed surprised to see the beautiful animal. "I am the most splendid creature in the entire animal kingdom," boasted the peacock. Now Gavin was beginning to dis-like the bird, "Oh, what a proud animal he is," he thought. He flew to meet his friends and said, "He is a beautiful bird indeed, but he brags a lot!" "So now you know how we feel when you brag as well," cried all the animals. Gavin learnt his lesson and never bragged again.

18 Dragon Hatchlings

Papa Dragon was guarding the three eggs while Mama Dragon had gone to search for food. Papa Dragon had spread out his wings to protect the eggs. He appeared very large and scary. One of the eggs began to crack but Papa Dragon didn't notice it as he was too busy guarding them. A pair of eyes looked outside and saw Papa Dragon. They were frightened at the sight of Papa Dragon. "Oh! What's that?" he cried. "It looks so scary. I'm not coming outside if I don't see my mother." The second egg also cracked and the sight of Papa Dragon also terrified the young hatchling inside. Mama Dragon returned with some food and saw that the eggs had hatched. She told Papa about it and he peeped inside the eggs. The young hatchlings were even more scared to see him from so close. Mama told them that their father was as soft as a pussycat from inside. They came out and licked their mother and father and soon realised that that Papa dragon was really as soft as a pussycat!

19 The Donkey Who Didn't Help

A dog and a donkey were walking along a mountain path to the market with their master. At noon, the master ate some food and then lay under a tree for a nap. The donkey fed on the grass that was growing there, but the poor dog had nothing to eat. He said to the donkey, "There are some buns in the load you are carrying. Let's have some of them." But the donkey told him to wait for the master to wake up. Just then a hungry wolf appeared. The donkey was trembling with fear and pleaded to the dog to help him. And the dog said, "I don't have any energy to help you as I've not eaten anything. Wait till the master gets up. He'll help you." But before that, the wolf attacked the donkey and made a meal of him. Donkeys really can be foolish!

20   The Three Billy Goats

There once lived three billy goats. They wanted to graze on grass. The grass grew on the mountainside. But they had to cross a little tunnel to reach the mountain. Inside this tunnel lived a wicked wolf that ate up all those who entered the tunnel. But the clever goats did not fear the wolf. The smallest billy goat went first and as he stepped inside the tunnel, the wolf shouted, "Who dares to enter my home?" "I am the smallest billy goat," came the reply. "I shall eat you up," growled the wolf.

"Please wait, for a bigger goat is on its way," said the small billy goat. The greedy wolf agreed to let him go.

The second billy goat also escaped the wolf in this manner. The wolf was becoming impatient. On seeing the third billy goat, the wolf pounced on him. "You cannot escape me!" he snarled. But the last goat was big and strong. He knocked the wolf down with his huge horns and killed it.

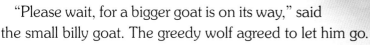

21   The Hungry Monkeys

A monkey trainer loved his monkeys. He took good care of them and fed them well. Once a famine followed a severe drought in the country they lived in. There was no food anywhere, except for a chestnut tree. The trainer decided to give the monkeys chestnuts until the famine ended. He gave each monkey two chestnuts. The monkey's were furious and created a huge uproar. They leapt around and yelped at the top of their voices. When the trainer tried to keep them quiet, they screamed even louder. Finally, the trainer understood what the monkeys were trying to communicate. They said they would die if they had to live on two chestnuts a day. The trainer felt sorry for his monkeys and decided to give each monkey a dozen chestnuts instead.

22 Oscar the Otter

Oscar the otter lay on the banks of the river to dry his wet fur. Some young birds flocked around Oscar and started laughing. "Look at his fur, they look like thorns!" "You look messy," joked another bird. Oscar was very angry at the birds and growled at them. The frightened birds ran towards the river and fell into it one by one. They cawed for help and fluttered their wings. Oscar laughed aloud, "Look at your-selves, you silly birds. Your feathers resemble spikes and you also have moss hanging from your faces!" Mama bird, who was watching all this from the branch, scolded them, "Look what happens when you make fun of someone else. His fur looks like thorns because it is wet. You must remember that otters eat all the marshy plants in the river and help keep the water clean," she explained. The birds understood their mistake and apologised to Oscar.

23 Blackberries and the Mouse

Paws the cat decided to chase Martin the mouse. So Martin started searching for a safe place to hide. Soon, he found a blackberry bush and hid behind it. The bush smelt good and he plucked a berry. "The berries taste so sweet," said Martin and licked his lips. He ate berries till his stomach was full and he could hardly move. After a while, he went to sleep. Meanwhile, Paws came looking for Martin. When he went closer to the bush, he heard someone snoring. It was Martin! Paws crouched low and pounced on him but Martin was quicker. He sprang up the nearby tree. Paws too climbed up the tree but Martin was sitting at the edge of the branch. Paws knew that if he went further, the branch would break. He shook the branch up and down to make Martin fall but Martin clutched the branch as hard as he could. Tired of shaking the branch, Paws gave up and left the place. After sometime, Martin came down the tree and ran back to his mouse hole where he could be safe and fell asleep dreaming of blackberries.

24   I Didn't Do That

Two cats, Fluffy and Stripes, disliked Speedy the mouse. They lived in a huge house and were angry whenever Speedy came to nibble at their food. One night, when Fluffy and Stripes were fast sleep near the fireplace, Speedy popped out of his hole and went into the kitchen. There, he saw a large chunk of cheese and jumped with joy. He quickly climbed onto the table and started to eat. When he had finished, an idea dawned on him. "Why not teach these wicked cats a lesson?" he thought. He created a mess in the kitchen and made a trail of breadcrumbs from the kitchen to the fireplace. Next morning, when the owner of the house saw the mess, he was furious. Thinking that the cats had dirtied the place, he threw Fluffy and Stripes out of the house. While the cats shed tears, Speedy laughed aloud.

25   Troublesome Rhino

A group of animals lived in the jungle. They were all on peaceful terms with one another.

One day, a rhino entered the forest and said to the lion, "I wish to join your group."

When the lion asked him what were his special qualities, the rhino said that he could charge and trample everyone with his sharp horn. "We don't need you in that case. We don't want anyone who creates trouble," said the elephant. The rhino walked away from there in disgust. A little later, the animals heard a loud scrunch. They saw that the rhino's horn had got stuck in a tree trunk and he was pleading for help. The elephant agreed to help him on the condition that the rhino would promise never to charge through the jungle again. The rhino agreed and the elephant pulled out his horn with his trunk.

After that day, the rhino used his horn only for pulling out fruits for other monkeys and parrots.

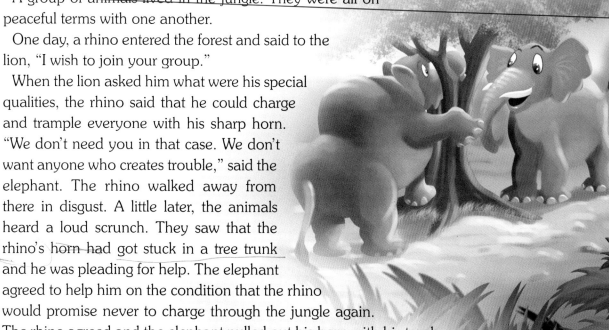

26 Tale of the Bunny Family

Benjamin Bunny married Flopsy Bunny and they had a large family of little bunnies. Sometimes when there were not enough cabbages to spare, they would gather things from the rubbish heap across the field. One day, they found some overgrown lettuce in the rubbish heap. They stuffed themselves with so much lettuce that the little bunnies felt drowsy and fell into a deep slumber in the grass. But Benjamin was not as drowsy as his children. After sometime, the sound of the mowing machine was heard from Mr. McGregor's lawn and the machine was approaching the place where the Bunnies lay asleep. Thomasina, an old little mouse woke Benjamin Bunny. While they were talking, they heard a heavy tread above their heads and a sackful of lawn mowings fell on the sleeping bunnies. Benjamin Bunny protected himself with a paper bag while the mouse herself hid in a pot. The little rabbits continued to sleep. They were dreaming that their mother was tucking them in a bed of hay.

Mr. McGregor dropped a sack on the bunnies and took them home. He placed the sack near the wall. Thomasina bit the sack with her sharp teeth and out came the little bunnies. Benjamin and Flopsy stuffed rubbish inside the sack and took their babies away.

When Mr. McGreogor opened the sack in front of his wife to show her the little bunnies, she was furious. All it had were inside were old bottles, cans and old boots!

27 Three Naughty Mice

Three naughty mice lived in a hole on the ground floor of a house. The owners of the house, Mr. and Mrs. Bubnoggin, kept jars full of jellybeans and sourballs on the kitchen counter. They didn't realise that the three mice stole the sweets each night after they had gone to bed. One night, when Mr. Bubnoggin went to the kitchen to take a sourball, he was astonished to see the three mice busy eating the sweets. He picked up the mice by their tails and threw them out of the window. But the mice soon found their way back into the house. Mrs. Bubnoggin put some cheese shreds on a saucer next to the jars. But the mice didn't even touch the cheese and only nibbled on the sourballs. Now Mrs. Bubnoggin put some sweets along with the cheese. The next morning, they were relieved to see that the mice had not touched the jars of sweets but had only nibbled away on the food kept for them. From then on, Mrs. Bubnoggin left food for the mice every day.

28 The Boastful Crow

A crow ridiculed a flock of geese, "You don't even know how to fly. All you know is how to flap your wings." The geese decided to challenge the crow. "Let us have a competition to see who flies better," they said. The crow displayed his flying skills, swooping, gliding and circling and somer-saulting in the air. One of the geese started to fly above the sea. The crow flew after him, passing rude comments along the way. They flew endlessly till land was out of sight. Now the crow began to tire. But he knew that if he stopped flying he would fall in the sea and drown. At last when he could no longer fly, he asked the goose to help him. The goose took pity on him and carried him on his back to the shore. The crow realised that his boasting had taught him a lesson.

29 Brer Rabbit and the Tar Baby

Once, a fox made a toy baby out of tar and called it the Tar Baby. He made it wear a cap and placed it on the road. Then he hid behind the bush to see what would happen. Soon Brer Rabbit passed that way. He wished the Tar Baby good morning. But when the Tar Baby did not respond after being greeted several times, Brer Rabbit became angry. He punched it on the face and obviously his hand got stuck. Soon both his feet were also stuck in the tar. The fox had a good laugh at the sight. When Brer Rabbit saw the fox, he yelled, "You can roast me up but please do not throw me into the Brer patch! Anything but the patch!" Now, the fox thought that the Brer patch must be a dangerous place and so he threw the rabbit there. But to his surprise, the rabbit was safe. Clever Brer Rabbit laughed and said, "I was born and brought up in this patch!" He laughed and escaped.

30 Uneasy Neighbours

A mongoose, a cat, an owl and a rat lived in a banyan tree. The rat and the mongoose lived in their holes at the bottom of the tree, the cat lived halfway up the tree while the owl stayed on the top branches. Everyone was afraid of the cat but the rat was fearful of all the animals. One day, the cat was caught in a hunter's trap. Her neighbours were relieved to see her in this situation, as now they would have no one to fear. The rat saw the mongoose approaching him and knew that only the cat could keep away the mongoose. So, the clever rat nibbled on the net and made a big hole in it. The cat rushed out from the net and seeing him, the mongoose and the owl also fled. The rat also fled. By saving the cat, he had saved his own life.

31 Stealing Eggs

Curly the Chipmunk stole eggs from other animals' nests and was eager to eat them. Murdock the mouse told him not to destroy other animals' nests and steal their eggs as it would get her into trouble one day. But Curly laughed off Murdock's warnings and ate her supper of roasted grasshoppers, ladybugs, beetles and scrambled eggs. The next morning, Curly was hungry again. She thought about the eggs she had eaten and wanted somemore. Soon Murdock saw Curly behind a bush carrying six, white quail eggs. A little while later, Curly came back with a huge egg. Murdock was surprised to see such a big egg and asked Curly from where he got it. "I found it in a nest on the ground," replied Curly. "It must be a crocodile's egg or an ostrich's. They are big and can knock you off," said Murdock. "Ha! There are no crocodiles or ostriches here, you silly mouse," chuckled Curly. Soon Curly heard a hustling sound behind the bushes. Murdock tried to frighten him by saying that the animal had come to take its egg back. "Who is there? Get away! You can't take away my egg!" And just then an owl darted forth. Curly was so afraid that he dropped the egg to the ground. The owl immediately picked it up and flew back to its nest. "I told you never to steal another animal's eggs. You're lucky that the owl didn't attack you with its talons," said Murdock. From that day, Curly stopped stealing eggs from other animals' nests.

Contents

The Story of the Month

The Story of the Blue Jackal

01 The Story of the Blue Jackal

Jackie, a young jackal lived with his friends in a forest. It was a dry summer and there was hardly any food for the animals to eat. Driven by hunger, Jackie went to the nearby village in search of food. "I hope I find a fat hen for a sumptuous meal," prayed Jackie and hid behind the bushes outside a washerman's hut. Suddenly a herd of mongrels came rushing towards Jackie. Quite frightened, Jackie ran into the courtyard and plop! fell headlong into a vat full of blue dye which the washerman had kept for bleaching the clothes. Alas! Jackie's fur turned blue! When he came out, he was a blue animal and thinking he was not the jackal they were chasing, the mongrels left.

The jackal went back to the forest. Seeing his weird appearance, all the animals including the lion and the tiger ran away from him. "Why don't I take advantage of my new appearance and lead a good life?" thought Jackie and announced, "I'm a special creature send by God to rule over you. The animals believed him and accepted him as their ruler. Jackie appointed the lion and the tiger as his ministers and the wild bear as his gatekeeper, but banished all the jackals from the forest for fear of being identified. Everyday the animals hunted and brought food for their king. Jackie in turn had his share and distributed the rest among the other animals. Life had never been so comfortable. "My blue colour has indeed turned out to be a blessing," thought Jackie.

One day as Jackie was resting under the shade of the Oak tree guarded by the lion, the tiger and the bear, he heard a very familiar howl. "Seems like my friends are looking for me," thought Jackie and without even realising what he was doing, he howled out "Hoooooaaaaa…" "Our ruler is no one special but a jackal," shouted the lion. "Kill this imposter," shouted the other animals who had heard Jackie's howl and gathered around. The terrified jackal fled for his life and the animals chased him out of the forest.

02 How Do I Get to the Top?

Bobo the monkey lived in a deep jungle. One day, while it was raining, he spotted a banana tree high up the mountains but the only way to reach it was by climbing up the waterfall. "I want to eat the bananas! What shall I do?" he wondered. Bobo decided that he would make his way up the vines hanging from the trees. He caught hold of one of the vines and thought, "This is easy!" But as he swung to catch hold of another vine, his hands slipped and he came down tumbling. Thud! Crash! "What do I do now?" wondered Bobo. He tried climbing the rocks but came down again. "Oh!" he moaned. Then he saw his friend, the parrot. "Will you carry me up the mountain if I cling onto your feet?" The parrot replied, "You are too heavy, but we can try." As they flew, the parrot could not carry so much weight and the monkey fell down. Soon, the rain stopped and there were only few drops trickling down the waterfall. "Now is my chance," thought Bobo. Finally, he was able to climb up and eat delicious bananas till his tummy almost burst.

03 The Swan Bride

A woman lived with her daughter and stepdaughter. One day, God appeared in the guise of a poor old man in their house. The woman and her daughter behaved rudely with him. But the stepdaughter welcomed him warmly and offered him water. God cursed the woman and her daughter turning them as black as crows. But he blessed the stepdaughter and turned her into an extremely beautiful maiden. One day, the king happened to see the beautiful maiden while he was passing by in his chariot. He was overwhelmed by her beauty and wished to marry her. When the woman and her stepdaughter heard this, they became jealous and pushed the fair maiden into a river where she turned into a swan. The king's hunters caught the swan and brought it to the palace. As soon as the swan stepped into the palace, it was transformed to its original form. The king married the lovely maiden and punished the dark mother and daughter.

04 The Dove and the Lion

Long back in a dense jungle, there lived a white dove. Every day, the dove used to fly to far off places to search for food grains. One day, some wicked hunters spotted the dove feeding on grains in a field. One of the hunters said to another, "Look! How beautiful the dove is. I will make it my pet." He ran after the dove, but it managed to escape. After flying for a long time, the dove spotted a cave but she didn't see a lion hiding inside it. As soon as the dove felt she was safe inside, the lion pounced upon her and ate her up.

That is why the wise say—in avoiding one evil, one must take care not to fall into another.

05 The Ass's Brains

Once, there lived a clever fox. He used to stay and roam around with the king of the jungle, the lion. One day, the lion was very hungry. He asked, "Oh fox! What use is your cleverness if it cannot get me my prey easily?" The fox replied, "Ok, I will get some food for you but you must do as I say. You have to tell the ass that you are going to make him your brother." The lion agreed. The ass was overjoyed at this invitation and went to meet the lion. As the lion saw him standing, he pounced on him and killed him. Suddenly, the lion felt thirsty. So he told the fox to guard the ass's body while he went to drink some water. The fox could not wait and ate up the ass's brains. When the lion came back and saw the brain missing, he roared, "Who ate this?" The fox very cleverly replied back, "Oh King! The ass never had any brains!"

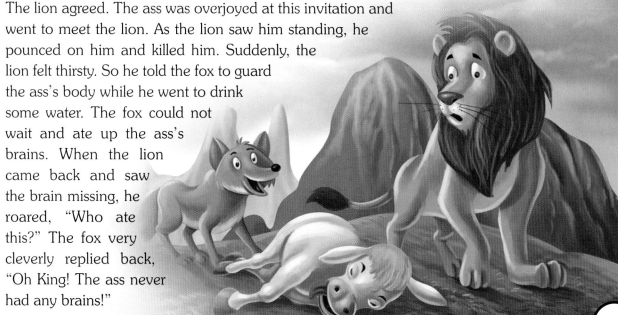

06 Real Friends Help Each Other

Once, in a jungle near a big deep pond, there lived three furry beavers, Digger, Flap and Castor. Once, while they were sleeping inside their lodge, a frog started croaking outside. Digger said, "Oh! I wish someone would tell this frog to keep quiet!" "I am too tired," said Flap. Castor got up from his couch and slipped out into the icy water of the pond. He shouted, "Oh dear Frog, please do not croak near our lodge." The frog knew the beavers and went away. Soon Castor noticed that it was a bright, sunny day. He shouted, "Hey, come out and enjoy the weather." Digger and Flap came out to join Castor. As they enjoyed the lovely weather, Digger got an idea. "My friends," he said, "yesterday I noticed a leak in our lodge. Let us repair that leak before it gets wider." Digger decided to cut the tree while Flap and Castor gathered twigs. But as they finished cutting, an eagle started flying over them and they rushed back inside. Next day, the beavers started repairing their lodge. An otter and a squirrel, who were watching them joined in to help them. After sometime, the eagle came too. By now the lodge was repaired and the beavers invited everybody for a feast.

07 The Tortoise That Refused to Leave Home

Once upon a time in a big city, there was a river with many fishes and tortoises. Once, it so happened that there were no rains and everybody feared a drought. All the fishes and tortoises started moving to other ponds and lakes. Among them, there was a tortoise who didn't want to go. His friend said, "Let's go! This river will dry and you will die." The tortoise was very stubborn and said, "No I will not go anywhere, this is my home." And he stayed back. When all his friends left, he dug a hole in the clay on the riverbed and closed himself in. One day a potter came to the river to dig out clay to make pots. Alas! He hit that very place with his spade where the tortoise was resting. The spade hit the shell and it broke. Before dying, the tortoise said, "I have learnt the lesson that home is where all our loved ones are."

08 Finlay and His Pot of Honey

Once there lived two big brown bears named Finlay and Janet. During the chilly winters, they used to stay inside their cave. Both of them slept throughout the winter. One day, Finlay woke up and was overjoyed to see that spring had arrived. Every nook and corner was blossoming with flowers. "Janet! Wake up! Look, spring is here." Janet was also happy, "I am going to the river to catch some fish," she announced. Finlay scowled and said, "I want to eat honey!" After searching for a long time, Finlay spotted a beehive on top of a tree. He climbed up the tree and hit the beehive. While the bees flew away, Finlay collected the honey in a pot. "Look Janet! I got some honey! Let us feast on it," he said. Both of them drank to their full and rested. When Finlay came out for some more honey, the bees were waiting to attack him. Finlay saw the bees and ran towards the river to save himself. Meanwhile, Janet finished all the honey. When Finlay came back, he ate some berries and decided never to steal honey again.

09 An Eagle's Sore Eyes

Alasdiar, the eagle, was flying high up in the air. Suddenly, a small piece of fur went into his left eye. He rubbed his eye but could not take the fur out. Soon his eye started paining. Just then, he spotted Barden the snake sunbathing on a rock. "This would be a perfect meal," thought Alasdiar as he lifted the snake in his beak. Soon, his eye started paining again and when he began to rub it, the snake slipped away. Alasdiar was very angry. Just then he saw Blossom, the squirrel, and thought of eating her instead. But this time Blossom's furry tail tickled his eye and the squirrel escaped. Alasdiar was sad, "Let me wash my eyes with water," he thought. In the river, he saw lots of fishes and caught some of them and was very happy once again.

141

10 The Jackdaw and the Doves

There was a greedy jackdaw who lived in a thick jungle. One day, as he was flying over the fields, he saw a big colony of doves feeding over grains. These doves had a lot of food grains. The jackdaw wondered, "Why are these doves so lucky? They have so much to eat. I will live with them." So he painted himself white so that the doves would not recognise him. In the beginning, the jackdaw ate silently. But after some days, he started talking to other doves. As soon as the doves came to know about the real nature of the jackdaw, they drove him away. The jackdaw was very upset. The other jackdaws didn't recognise him any more since he was now white. Alas! He didn't have any friend now.

11 The Fox and the Monkey King

Long ago there lived many animals in a jungle. Once a year all the animals gathered under a huge rock to elect their king who would rule the jungle. This year was no different. All the animals gathered around the rock. Everybody cast their vote. The monkey was chosen as the king of all the animals because everyone found his antics amusing. Everybody accepted him except the fox. The fox sulked, "I am cleverer than that monkey, so how has he become the king?" One day, he found a trap on a jungle path. The fox decided to fool the monkey and placed the trap below the tree in which the monkey lived. Tempted by the bananas that the fox held out to him, the monkey fell right into the trap. The fox exclaimed, "Ha! You cannot take care of yourself, how will you rule the jungle?"

12   The Mischievous Kitten

Plum was a naughty little kitten, always full of life. Mrs. Glen, her mistress, was always scolding her for her naughtiness. Mrs. Glen loved knitting. One afternoon, while she was busy knitting a woollen scarf, she fell asleep. Plum ran towards the couch where Mrs. Glen had placed her wool. "Wow! That's a nice ball," thought Plum and slowly picked up a ball of wool in her mouth. She hopped and jumped all around the room. Her legs got entangled in the wool. She couldn't move. Plum struggled to free herself but failed. "Meeww…" Plum cried aloud. Mrs. Glen woke up with a jerk. "Oh, you naughty kitty…look what you've done to my wool!" she shouted. Plum wailed in dismay. Mrs. Glen took pity on Plum and disentangled her. Then she gave her a stern look and said, "This serves you right, Girl." Plum was pale with fear and promised never to play with wool again.

13   Why Does the Buffalo Walk Slowly?

A long time ago, the buffalo and hare were great friends. They used to run very fast. It became very difficult to decide who was the faster of the two. One day, they both decided to have a race and end the argument. The hare started running as fast as he could. But the buffalo also ran fast and went past the hare. The hare was worried and thought, "If the buffalo runs so fast he will win the race. I must do something to stop him." So he went to the buffalo and told him, "My friend slow down, the whole earth is trembling under your weight. I fear if you do not stop running, the earth will sink taking us all under." The buffalo heard this and slowed down and the hare won the race. From that day onwards, the buffalo walks slowly.

14 Joe the Dog of the Year

Joe was running towards Dolly's house when he saw the 'Dog of the Year Award' notice. He rushed to tell Dolly about it. She was standing outside her house reading the same notice on her fence. Dolly was sure that the award belonged to her. "Joe doesn't stand a chance of winning this award," she thought. She glanced at Joe, turned her nose up and went inside her house. Joe was surprised at her odd behaviour.

Dolly was his best friend. He couldn't live without her. A few days later, Joe was at the award ceremony with his master, Andy. He was dozing off when suddenly he heard his name. "Ladies and Gentleman! The award for the Dog of the Year goes to Joe." Joe was startled. What a pleasant surprise! Andy gave him a tight hug and said, "I was sure that you would win. You're the best dog anyone can have." And guess what! Dolly came and licked his face. She couldn't stay away from Joe either, after all.

15 The Clever Hare and the Lion

Once there lived a lion who was the king of a jungle. One day, he declared to the other animals, "Everyday I want one animal killed and offered to me else you will all have to leave the jungle." Many animals were sacrificed. Soon it was the turn of a clever hare. All night, he thought of how to get out of this difficult situation. Suddenly he hit upon a clever idea.

The next day, he went to the lion's den. The hare said gently, "O' King, there is another lion in a well who is calling you weak and foolish." Hearing this, the lion growled in anger and vowed to kill his rival. The clever hare led him to a well filled with water. When the lion peeped in, he saw his own reflection in the water. The foolish lion thought it to be the enemy and jumped into the well and got drowned. From that day, all the animals lived in peace and without fear.

16 Bullies Never Win

Gregor was a big fat mouse who used to bully around the other mice of the glen. Innes was one of his victims. Everyday Gregor would shout at Innes and Innes would run to the woods in search of food for Gregor. One day Gregor shouted, "Innes, you lazy little mouse, where are you? Get me some cheese! If you do not go now, I will hang you up on the tree by your tail!" Innes was terrified, "Gregor, please don't do that! I am going," he pleaded. As he was looking around for cheese, Elspeth the butterfly came along. "Why do you look so sad?" Tired and hungry, Innes replied, "I am searching for cheese for that big fat bully Gregor. He always makes me hunt for his food." Elspeth heard Innes's sad woes. She said, "Today will be the last day of Gregor's bullying. Go into that shed. It has cheese. I know a cat who can teach Gregor a good lesson." Innes went back and called out to Gregor. As soon as Gregor came out, Archibald the big cat, pounced on him. "I heard you bully Innes!" yelled the cat. Gregor trembled with fear and promised never ever to bully anyone again.

17 Summertime Watermelons

It was summertime. The best time for all the animals because they could now steal into Mrs. Gilbertson's garden and eat juicy watermelons. Her watermelons were the best. Mrs. Gilbertson's garden had already been ransacked when Noggy, the cub bear came along. He saw all animals eating watermelons. Some of the animals's face and fingers were red with the flesh of the watermelons. Noggy rushed back, "Mama, what is a watermelon? Can we eat it?" Mama Bear replied, "Yes dear, we will." Noggy rose early in the morning and went along with Mama Bear to Mrs. Gilbertson's garden. Lots of watermelons were lying around clinging to the vine. The Gopher family was already there, enjoying their share. Mama picked up one big juicy one, "Let's go, Noggy! We will eat in the woods, lest Mrs. Gilbertson sees us." In the woods, Mama cut the watermelon open and Noggy dug his fingers right into the watermelon. He ate till his tummy was full. Mama too enjoyed her share.

18 Hector the Hippo

Hector was a happy-go-lucky hippo. He loved to laze around in the river. All day he would lie in the muddy waters of the river. Hector had no worries in the world because he was the king of the river. A lion came near the river but the water was too cold for him. Then came the tiger, "Hector move aside, I want to lie in the river," he ordered. Hector slowly moved but the water was too cold and the tiger had to run away. Hector was happy to be the king of the river. Soon came a bird with a yellow belly. "Hector, can I fish in the river?" asked the bird. Hector said, "Sure, go ahead, there are lots of fish." The bird dipped its beak, got a fish and flew away. Hector lay snugly in the river undisturbed because he was the king of the river.

19 Country Mouse and Town Mouse

Once, a town mouse visited his brother in the countryside. They had a wonderful time in the meadows and farms. The town mouse invited his brother to the town. When the country mouse saw the town mouse's house, he was amazed to see so many things to eat! Suddenly, the owner of the house, Mrs. Polly, came into the kitchen and saw the mice nibbling at the cheese. She yelled so loudly that her husband came running. "Such nasty mice! I'm going to teach them a lesson," he said. In a moment, a huge brown cat chased the mice out of the kitchen. The country mouse said, "Brother, I am happy to see your house. You have many things to eat, but I would rather live safely in the country eating my simple meals than risk my life everyday." Saying this, the country mouse slipped away.

20 Edward the Bear

It was midnight in the jungle. Edward, the bear was sleeping in his bed. He had tucked himself snugly in his blanket for he knew the winter winds were blowing with all their might. A few hours later, Edward heard a scratching sound outside his window. It was very dark. A while later, he heard the same sound again. Edward rose from his bed and lit a candle. He gathered all his courage and opened his door to see who it was. "Who is knocking on my window?" he asked. No one replied. Suddenly the wind blew out his candle and it was dark. He heard the same sound again but this time he saw the tree branches scratching his window in the moonlight. Edward was relieved. He put out the candle and went back to sleep.

21 Catch Me If You Can

Rupert was a furry friendly otter. He loved playing with his blue ball. He would throw the ball high in the air and catch it when it came down. The higher the ball went, the happier he was. Once, he gathered all his strength and threw the ball really high. But this time it didn't land on the ground. Rupert waited, "Oh! Where is my ball?" he wondered. He asked a blue bird, "Have you seen my blue ball?" The blue bird replied, "No, but do check in the tall grass." Rupert searched but didn't find his ball. He asked a black spider but to no avail. Rupert asked the fish and they replied, "No, Rupert, there is no ball in the river. We didn't hear it splash either." Rupert stood under a tall tree and looked up. There high above, he saw his ball stuck between two branches! He asked a bird to throw it down. The bird helped him but warned him to be careful next time. Rupert decided never to throw his ball so high again.

22 Bacon and Eggs

Farmer Fred bred chickens and pigs. He fed them corn. One day he went to the market and bought five piglets. "I will give them corn so that they grow fat and I can have more bacon." Early next morning he came to the pigsty with a bowlful of corn for them. All the five piglets came running. When he had gone, a chicken said, "Do not eat the corn. You will become fat and the farmer will eat you!" The piglets stopped eating and hid in different places. After his afternoon nap, Fred came and found the corn bowl untouched. He sat down on a little rock, but the rock moved and instead of a rock there was a piglet! He locked it in the pigsty. Then Fred went fishing. As he was hooking his rod, the worm slipped into the river. Fred tried to catch the worm but instead his hands found a piglet. In the garden, he found three more piglets. Now, Fred had caught them all. This time the hungry piglets ate all the corn. Soon they became fat. One morning, the chicken smelled fresh bacon from Fred's kitchen. He knew who had been fried!

23 A Fair Race

One day, the lion called all the animals saying, "Let's have a race! Whoever wins will be given free food." Each animal was placed at different starting points. Animals like the tortoise were placed first as compared to the faster animals. The lioness was the judge. Soon, the race began. Some hours went by when suddenly there was a thundering noise and a gust of wind blew past the lioness. As the dust settled, she saw an antelope finishing first. The antelope had won. Suddenly the cheetah shouted, "Wait, I am the real winner, I had crossed the line. But in the hurry I did not notice the line and went ahead." Finally, the lioness gave her verdict, "Being fast is of no use if you cannot stop at the right place and at the right moment. So, I declare the antelope the winner!"

24   Waiting for the Rains

Summers are a tough time for animals in the Savannahs. All the rivers dry up. In the jungle, all the animals crowded around the little puddle that was left of the river. But the lions were not letting anybody past. Tambika, the elephant and her baby, Onoori, watched the lions with sad eyes. They were waiting to soak their muddy bodies in the river but the lions would not let them come near. Onoori screeched, "Mama, I want to go in the water." Mama sadly replied, "Onoori, we must wait for the rains to come. Do not worry. The dry season is ending because when the winds blow, the rainy season is round the corner." Next morning, Tambika woke up to find the air heavy. "Wake up, Onoori! Look up!" To Onoori's delight, there were dark clouds all over the sky. A little droplet fell on his face followed by another. Soon, it was pouring heavily. All the animals were happy because the river was full again.

25   Benny Bear's Birthday Cake

Benny was a little bear who always looked forward to birthdays because he loved his Mama's cakes. On his birthday, Benny woke up early and said, "Mama, make me a big cake today!" Mama took a huge pan, poured ten dozen eggs, fifty pounds of flour, milk, vanilla and sugar into it and mixed it well. She stood on a chair and stirred hard with a big shovel. The cake took five hours to bake. Once it was ready, Mama laid it on the kitchen table for icing. She topped it with vanilla and sugar till the icing trickled down the sides of the cake. Then she called Benny. He was delighted at the sight of such a huge cake. He jumped and landed right in the middle of the cake splattering the cream on Mama's face. Mama and Benny enjoyed eating the cake till their tummies ached. Benny kissed Mama, "Thanks, Mama! This is the best birthday cake I've ever had!"

26 Sharing an Easter Basket

Easter was a busy time for Jamie the bunny rabbit. He had to paint all the Easter eggs. "Why are you doing all this alone?" asked a canary sitting nearby. "I am not alone. My job is just to paint the eggs. Jack will be gifting them." "From where do you get these colours?" she asked. Jamie replied, "I get these colours from different flowers." At last the canary took her leave. "I will go now. You know, I have never received any Easter eggs," she said and flew away. When Jack came to collect the eggs, he left some for Jamie. As Jamie sat down to have his Easter eggs, he remembered the little canary. He packed a basket and left it under the tree to give her a surprise. The canary was delighted. She too collected berries and some of the best carrots for the bunny. Both of them exchanged gifts and had a happy Easter.

27   The Gardener and the Donkey

John had a big farm. Every week he went to the market to get more seeds and manure for his garden. John would always take his donkey along to carry the load. But every time he overloaded his donkey.

Once he went to the market and got huge sacks of manure. On the way back home, he loaded his donkey as usual. The climb to the town was steep. Along the way, John saw some wood and thought, "This would be useful in my garden." He placed some logs on the donkey saying; "This is hardly any weight."

After sometime, he came across some sugarcane fields. "Let me have one or two," he thought aloud and loaded the donkey again. After climbing for a while, John felt hot and unbuttoned his coat. As he was about to place it on the donkey, the donkey collapsed and couldn't get up. John realised his mistake and was never ever unkind to his donkey again.

28   The Three Little Pigs, the Tomatoes and the Apples

In a valley lived three pigs and a wolf. The wolf was always scheming to eat the pigs. He tried to catch them many times but they always managed to escape. One day, he knocked at the pigs' door, "Hello, friends! I have come to tell you about the delicious tomatoes in Jack's farm. Come out! I will take you there," he said. The pigs replied, "Thank you, friend! Come back at five o' clock in the evening. We will go with you." As soon as the wolf left, the pigs went to the farm and brought a huge basket of ripe red tomatoes. The wolf was annoyed. But he tried his luck again. "Come, let's go to the farm to pick apples!" the wolf invited the pigs. We will meet you at six o' clock," said the pigs. This time, the wolf arrived at the farm at five o' clock. But the pigs were already up in the tree. When they saw the wolf, they threw the apples at him and the wolf had to run away.

29 There's Something in the Lake!

One evening, a donkey, a deer and a beaver were swimming together in a small lake. It had been a while since they had been swimming. Now it was getting dark. Suddenly the deer shouted, "Something bit me, I think there is something in the water, let's get out." The donkey also felt a slight pull on his tail and shouted, "Oh! I think there is a monster in this lake, let's get out!" The beaver too felt a nip on his tail. He added, "Friends, this lake is haunted!" And they all got out of the water. When all three had left, a naughty bear swam out of the lake from the far corner. He chuckled aloud to himself, "Ha! Ha! Ha! It was fun scaring them." After that evening, whenever the bear saw these three together, he always smiled to himself.

30 The Mouse and the Douglas-fir Cone

A plump mouse used to live in a forest. Near the mouse's hole, lived a fox who was always on a lookout to eat the mouse. In fear of being eaten up, the mouse seldom used to leave the hole. One day, the mouse was very hungry and gathered courage to venture out of his hole. "I'll die without food!" he moaned. But as soon as he came out, the fox started following him.

The mouse ran as fast as he could, but the fox was faster. The mouse knew his end was near unless he found a hiding place. Suddenly, he spotted a Douglas-fir cone, with prickly spikes all around it, lying on the ground. Though he was able to escape through it, one of his legs got stuck in the prickly spikes. To this very day, the mouse's feet can be seen sticking out of the cone and so the legend lives.

31 Rain, Rain, Go Away!

Marib was a happy-go-lucky monkey who lived in the jungle. All day long he would jump from one tree to another, swinging by his tail and gobbling bananas. He loved the big green trees in the jungle, for this was his sweet home!

One fine sunny morning, Marib was sitting on a banana tree chomping delicious bananas. He looked down at the other animals grazing in the lush, greenfield below. He saw goats bleating and running here and there in fright. "Thank God, I am not a goat, otherwise I would have been always afraid of being eaten up by a lion." Then Marib saw some camels chewing acacia leaves and pitied them for having to eat prickly leaves. "I am happy the way I am. Whenever I am hungry I can easily move from one tree to another picking my choice of fruits and watch all the animals sitting atop the tree!"

Marib was about to eat another banana, when he heard a great noise. He looked up and saw the big grey clouds thundering aloud. "Let me gather some more bananas before the rains start splashing down on the ripe fruits," he thought and quickly jumped from branch to branch gathering some ripe bananas. A while later, it started raining heavily. All the animals started running for shelter. The goats cried for help and ran to the nearby caves. The poor camels got wet and all the birds came back to their nests, fluttering their colourful wings. The anthills were washed away too. All the poor little red ants got drenched! Marib covered himself with a big banana leaf and prayed that the rain would stop soon. "God, please save these poor animals!" he cried. After a few hours the rain slowed down, but the rivers were flooded and the earth was all wet. The ants started looking for a new place to build their home all over again. Marib shook off the leaf and climbed down. He was thankful that he lived on trees.

Contents

The Story of the Month: The Tale of the Brave Cat

September

The Story of the Month

The Tale of the Brave Cat

01 The Tale of the Brave Cat

Chloe was a little girl. She had no friends but loved animals, especially cats. On her tenth birthday, her father took her to an animal shelter where there were many cats. "You can chose a cat to take home, Chloe," said her father. Chloe was over-joyed! She hugged her father and said, "Oh! This is my best gift ever." Chloe liked all the cats at the shelter, but fell in love with a particular cat who had big, bright eyes. "I'll take her," Chloe said and named her Star. In a few days time, Star became very naughty. When Chloe was around she was good, but the moment she left for school, Star got down to her tricks. She tore the curtains, clawed the seats, lapped up all the milk in the kitchen and often stole fish. Chloe's parents were very angry. One day, they told Chloe that they would return Star to the shelter, if she did not learn to behave.

Chloe was very worried, she did not know how to tame Star. Then one day, Star gave birth to kittens. They mewed and waved their tiny paws. From that day, everything changed. Star was no longer a naughty cat. She took good care of her kittens. However, Chloe's parents were worried now that there were so many cats in the house. Every night when the kittens meowed, her father became very angry. One night, Star cried so loudly that everybody woke up. Chloe and her parents came rushing and saw Star running about frantically. Seeing Chloe, Star looked towards the kitchen and Chloe understood that her cat was trying to tell her something. Suddenly, they noticed a huge fire in the kitchen. "Hurry, let's go out!" screamed Chloe's father. "But what about the kittens?" asked Chloe. Chloe quickly grabbed Star and one kitten. There was no time to pick up the others and rushed out. But Star wriggled out and leapt back inside the house. Soon the fire brigade arrived. They warned everybody to stay at a safe distance from the house. "Please save my cat. She is inside!" pleaded Chloe. Suddenly, Star emerged with one kitten in her mouth. The firemen tried to stop her but she ran inside the house again. One by one she brought out six kittens, but her last baby was still inside. Star jumped inside as the flames engulfed the house. Chloe and her parents looked on anxiously. The firemen brought out their huge pipes and began spraying water. After almost an hour, the flames died. Everything was quiet, but still there was no sign of Star. Chloe cried inconsolably. She had lost her best friend. Suddenly her father exclaimed, "Look, Star!" Chloe looked up. One of the firemen emerged from the house with Star and her last kitten. Star's ears and fur were singed and she was limping. "She is a brave cat," said the fireman. "Indeed, she is," agreed Chloe's father. "Her screams alerted us all." "And she is a star all right!" quipped Chloe as she rushed to embrace her cat. The scared kittens snuggled around their mother, as all the neighbours gathered around to have a look at the brave cat.

02 The Red-Feathered Hen

Red Queen the hen had red feathers. One day, Toby the fox saw Red Queen and said, "I'm going to eat this hen for dinner." He said to his wife, "Keep the water boiling for a delicious chicken broth for dinner." Off went Toby to catch Red Queen. He hid behind a tree and waited for her to cross that way. "Too-doodle-doo… Sqawck!" sang Red Queen walking merrily. Toby grabbed her neck and shoved her into a sack. The hen's friend, the goose, saw what had happened. "I must help Red Queen," she thought.

The goose lay on the road, pretending to be injured. Seeing the injured bird, greedy Toby left the sack to catch the goose. To his surprise, the goose got up and ran farther and farther away. Toby chased after her. Red Queen took this opportunity to climb out of the sack and escape. She put a stone inside. Unable to catch the goose, Toby returned. "At least I have a hen for dinner," he thought. He picked up the sack and hurried home. He turned the sack over the pot of boiling water. "Splash!" The stone spilled hot water on the greedy fox and burned his paws!

03 A Clever Reply

One day the lion, the king of the jungle, called an important meeting at his den. The lion was very dirty and so was his den. Unable to bear the smell, the zebra covered his nose. "How dare you cover your nose? Does my den stink?" roared the lion. The zebra had no adequate reply and the lion threw him out of the den. The king then asked the elephant the same question. "No, it smells of roses," replied the frightened elephant. The lion wasn't happy with this reply either and knocked the elephant's trunk. He then asked the fox. "Sir, I have a cold so I cannot smell anything," replied the intelligent fox. The lion was happy with this clever reply and made the fox his minister.

04   The Dirty Pig

One fine day, a dirty pig was soaking himself in a pool. A thirsty lion came to drink water, but unable to bear the heavy stench went away. The foolish pig thought that the lion cowed down seeing him and excitedly challenged him to a duel. "Maybe tomorrow," replied the lion and turned away from the smelly pig. The pig went home and told his parents how he had challenged a coward lion. "What have you done you, foolish pig? It's not you but your stench that made him run away," explained his father. The dirty pig's excitement crashed instantly. His father suggested that he should leisurely roll in the dirty waters so that he might stink even more and then meet the lion. The pig listened to his father. As soon as the lion approached him, the foul smell spread around and he ran away unable to bear it. Since then, pigs always keep themselves dirty so that no animal might come near them.

05   Kangaroos Get a Pouch

Once upon a time, in the tall grasslands of Australia, a Mother Kangaroo used to live with her son, Joey. One fine day, Mama Kangaroo was worried that Joey had been missing for a while. She hopped to the tall bushes to search and bumped into an old wombat. "Oh! Who is this who cannot leave an old blind wombat alone?" thundered the wombat. Mama apologised and told him that she was in a hurry. Wombat pleaded, "Please help me, I am hungry." Mama told the wombat to hold her tail and she would take him to green pastures. Mama Kangaroo hopped with the old wombat behind and stopped where she saw the green grass so that the wombat could chew. The old wombat then asked, "Please can you take me to a river? I am thirsty." Mama, though worried about her son, again helped. As she went near the river, she saw little Joey sleeping near the riverside. She hopped to lift her baby and kissed him. The wombat turned into an angel and said to Mama Kangaroo, "Mama, you are the kindest of all animals. I had asked others too but nobody stopped." The angel asked the Mother Kangaroo to tie a bark of a tree around her tummy. As she did so, it turned into a pouch! Mama was overjoyed and lifted her Joey into the pouch. From that day onwards, all kangaroos have pouches.

06 The Hare and the Tortoise

Once there lived a hare and a tortoise. The proud hare always laughed at the slow-moving tortoise. But the patient tortoise replied, "I move slowly but I can beat you in a race." The hare laughed and thought, "I'll beat him in a few seconds." He agreed to run with the tortoise. The next day, the race began. As the hare advanced much ahead of the tortoise, he thought, "I can take a nap here and run again when the tortoise reaches my mark. Anyway I will win this race." When the tortoise passed by, he saw the hare sleeping. He smiled and continued on his way, slowly and steadily. The hare woke up later only to find that the tortoise had reached the finishing point and won the race! He repented for his boastful habit.

07 Angus the Tartan Goat

Once, there lived a goat named Angus. He stayed with his owners, Mr. and Mrs. Douglas. They pampered Angus like a baby. However, Angus loved chewing woollen clothes and his master and mistress scolded him for doing so. One morning, Mr. and Mrs. Douglas had to go to the market. Before leaving, they put Mr. Douglas' favourite woollen jacket on the clothesline. "Angus, don't chew the jacket," warned the Douglases. Once the Douglases left, it began to pour heavily. "Oh, the coat is getting wet! I must pull it down," thought Angus. However, even before he knew it, he was chewing the coat. When the rains stopped, Angus realised what he had done. "Oh no," he thought, "this time they will throw me out of the house." He decided to keep quiet about it. When the Douglases returned, Mr. Douglas asked, "Has the wind blown away my coat?" Angus promptly nodded. However, Mrs. Douglas noticed a strand of wool sticking against Angus' chin. "Why! It's the jacket wool," screamed Mrs. Douglas. "So you're the culprit," confirmed Mr. Douglas. Poor Angus had to go without his lunch and dinner. He swore never to chew wool again.

08 Half Educated

Once there lived a wolf and a jackal. One day, the wolf bragged to the jackal, "You are not even half as educated as me." The jackal quietly agreed, but suddenly a tiger roared, "Nobody is as educated as I am." The wolf froze seeing the tiger while the jackal quickly thought of a plan to escape. "Sure you are, Sir and, therefore, we were coming to you for help," replied the jackal. "We want you to decide who among the two of us should eat the chickens." "First show me the chickens," growled the tiger, who was thinking of savouring not only the chickens, but also the healthy jackal and the wolf. The jackal took him to a small cave and said, "Sir, you have to enter the cave to see the chickens." As soon as the greedy tiger went inside, the clever jackal covered the entrance with a huge boulder. "You might be more educated, but you are definitely not smarter than me!" called out the jackal. "I was wrong," acknowledged the wolf, "you are certainly cleverer than me."

09 The Cock's Ruse

On a summer afternoon when the Sun shone bright, all animals complained about the heat. The Sun felt very hurt. He stopped coming out, making the Earth cold and dark. The animals immediately sent their messenger, the cock to enquire. When asked the reason for not showing up, the Sun replied, "I shine throughout the day to give you light and all you do is complain about how hot I am. I refuse to shine again." "Which means I have to return home in the dark, while the wild cat prepares to pounce on me," lamented the cock. The cock flew away and after some time the Sun heard a loud call. Immediately, the Sun rose up and the entire Earth shone bright. However, the Sun could not find the cock anywhere. Since then, whenever the cock calls out, the Sun promptly shines bright.

10 The Stork and the Fox

Once upon a time, a stork and a fox lived in the jungle. The fox was very cunning and he loved to play tricks on the stork. One day, the fox invited the stork for dinner. "Brother Stork, please come for some delicious home-cooked food, tonight," the fox said.

In the evening, the stork went to visit the fox. The fox brought out a delicious-smelling soup on a flat plate. He placed the plate in front of the stork. While the stork had trouble sipping his soup, the fox lapped his share up and laughed at the stork. "You have been so gracious to me. I must return the favour," said the stork. "You are invited to dinner at my house tomorrow."

Then next day, when the fox came to visit the stork, she served him cooked fish in a pitcher. While the stork happily ate her fish with her long beak, the fox was left whining and hungry. The cunning fox had learnt his lesson and stopped playing tricks on the stork.

11 The Goat and the Fox

A wily fox was once wandering in the forest. Unable to see a well in front of him, the fox fell into it. "Oh gracious me!" he thought. "I have to get out of the well before I die of cold." While he was thinking, a goat happened to pass by. "Mmm… the water in this well tastes so good!" said the fox loudly. The goat peered into the well and asked, "Is it really sweet?" asked the goat. "Jump in! I will help you come out of it later!" offered the fox. As soon as the goat jumped into the well, the fox climbed on him and got out of the well and ran away. The foolish goat lay there shivering!

12 Turn Out the Light

Three bears, Rick, Rusty and Coal were very scared of the dark. So every night they lit the street lamps and went to sleep. One day, a bear named Arthur came to stay in the neighbourhood. "Who dare keep the lights on at night?" he growled. One by one he switched off all the street lamps and threatened to beat up Rick, Rusty and Coal if they dared switch on the lights.

"We have to think of a plan to outsmart Arthur," declared Rusty. They all thought hard and at last, Coal hit on a plan. That night they surrounded Arthur's house with bulbs. Rick hid in the bushes and asked his friends to light all of them. Hearing a noise, Arthur woke up and opened his door. The bright light nearly blinded him and he tripped down the stairs. The three bears laughed and clapped their hands. "Don't you dare switch off the lights ever again or else…" they threatened Arthur. Groaning in pain, Arthur went back to his house. That night all the bears slept peacefully.

13 Tony the Lonely Goat

Tony was a very lonely goat. He was often seen roaming the mountains in search of a friend. One day, when he went to the river and saw a small goat in the water, he bleated joyfully, "Would you be my friend?" The fishes in the river laughed aloud, "You stupid goat, that's your reflection you're talking to!" Tony was surprised. While walking back home, tears welled up in his eyes and he thought, "I am so unlucky, I don't have any friend nor any siblings." As soon as he reached home, his father hugged him tight. "Welcome, Tony, see what we have here for you!" Tony hurriedly went to the backyard and saw a little white goat lying beside his mother. "That's your sister!" exclaimed his mother. Tony bleated happily, "I will never be lonely again!"

14 The Root of the Matter

One day, a hungry porcupine came to a dog to ask for food. The dog took the porcupine to a sugarcane field and asked him to eat to his heart's content. The hungry porcupine chewed away all the plants. The next morning, the owner noticed the dog near his garden and asked him if he had chewed the plants, "Sir, the porcupine is the culprit," confirmed the dog. When the porcupine was questioned he replied, "Sir, you should judge the matter when both of us are present. Will you wait till I get the dog here?" The man agreed. The porcupine waited for winter to set in. Then on a cold winter morning, accompanied by the dog, he went to the man's house to solve the case. When the man asked who the culprit was, the porcupine pointed at the dog. The poor dog could say nothing for his teeth kept chattering in the cold. The owner thinking this to be an admission of his guilt beat up the dog.

15 The Little Grey Donkey

The fair had come to the village after a long time. Everyone in the village was excited about it. The elders wanted to see the big games and the children ran to enjoy the different rides. But nobody came to the donkey man for rides. Raghu the donkey man was sad. "Alas! I will not be able to make a single penny. What will I gift my wife?" wondered Raghu. He waited for the children to come to him for rides.

The little grey donkey was watching all this. He loved his master very much. "How can I help my master?" he wondered. Then an idea struck him and he started to bray loudly. All the children were surprised to hear the noise and came running to the donkey. "What is he saying?" asked one child. Raghu joyfully said, "He is saying, come, ride me and see what fun it is!" Soon Raghu had many children queuing up to ride the donkey. He was very happy and so were the children.

16 Bright Eyes the Glider Possum

Bright Eyes was a possum, who lived with his parents. He used to live in his mother's pouch. As the days passed, he grew a furry coat, pink ears and nose and a fluffy tail. One fine day, Bright Eyes' mother climbed up a big tree on whose branches was hanging a big beehive. Bright Eyes popped his head out of the pouch and saw the big beehive. "What is that?" he asked his mother. His mother explained to him how he could collect the honey. After this, his father came and showed him how to glide. He asked Bright Eyes to expand his flying skin. This skin would help him keep afloat. He then held out his tail straight and leapt forward. Bright Eyes was very excited for now he could fly like a free bird. "Marvellous!" exclaimed his father who was watching his son joyfully. Bright Eyes went round and round then down and down and finally took a sharp curve and soared higher. "I can fly!" exclaimed Bright Eyes.

17 The Scorpion and the Frog

A scorpion lived in a dark and dingy cave near a mountain. He grew tired of his surroundings and wanted a change. One day, he came out of his cave and noticed that the valley across the river was very green. He crawled up to the riverbank and wondered how to cross it. Suddenly, he noticed a frog leaping around. "Hello, Mr. Frog, would you carry me to the other side of the river?" asked the scorpion. "I would have but you see I don't trust scorpions," replied the frog. "All scorpions are not bad. If I sting you on the way I will die for I do not know how to swim," explained the scorpion. Now the frog saw enough reason in the scorpion's statement and agreed to carry him across the river. So the scorpion hopped on to the frog's back and they set out on the journey. The frog paddled his limbs through the water as fast as he could. Half way through the journey, he suddenly felt a sharp sting on his soft hide. "Why did you sting me? Now both of us shall drown," cried he. "What can I do for this is my nature," replied the unrepentant scorpion. The frog and the scorpion immediately drowned in the gushing water.

18 Koobar the Koala and Water

Long ago, there was a young orphan boy named Koobar. He lived with his relatives in a dry country where water was seldom found. His relatives ill-treated him and never gave him enough water. Koobar was always thirsty. One day, when his relatives went out, Koobar drank all the water and not even a single drop was left. "Oh no! My relatives will come and beat me!" he thought. Koobar hit upon a plan. He quickly climbed a tall pine tree with all the buckets and sat there waiting for his relatives. Once they arrived and noticed that there was no water, they called out for Koobar. "There he is, hiding behind the branches on the pine tree!" cried one. "Come down or else we shall thrash you!" threatened another relative. They quickly climbed the tree and dragged Koobar to the ground. Then they beat him up with sticks. As tears rolled down his cheeks, the young boy prayed to God. Suddenly, he was transformed into a koala bear. Everybody was startled. Then Koobar announced, "From now on, if you cause any harm to me, I shall weave my magic charm and dry up all the water and you shall die of thirst!" That is why Koala bears are loved so much because everyone is scared that they might dry up all the water.

19 A Trunk Full of Clothes

Once upon a time, there lived a bear named Bartholomew who was loved by one and all in the jungle. One day, while Bartholomew went to the river to fish, he noticed a huge trunk. He nudged the cover and after much effort opened it. "What colourful clothes," he exclaimed. "There are caps, pants, shirts, suits!" Bartholomew quickly took out, a shirt, a hat and a pair of trousers. Once he was ready, he went to the river to see his reflection. Suddenly, the monkey noticed him and swooped down to enquire. Bartholomew showed him the trunk full of clothes. Soon word spread and all the animals gathered around Bartholomew. Each wanted something to wear. Soon a tussle broke out. They snatched, pulled, pushed and scratched. "Stop it!" screamed Bartholomew. All the clothes in the trunk were torn into pieces and none had anything to wear. "Can't help you because you had your chance as well," pointed Bartholomew and walked away.

20 Coloured

Long ago, the crow used to be a white bird. In his neighbourhood, lived an owl who had a dye shop. The crow was fascinated by the myriad colours. He flew down to the owl's shop and asked if his white body could be coloured. "I want to be the most beautiful bird in the world," he said. The owl agreed and asked him to come the next day. Now the owl was slightly blind but he was too vain to wear spectacles. While mixing the colours for the crow, he poured black instead of lilac. The crow arrived early the next day. "There you are!" said the owl "Your colours are ready. Just dive into that pool of water." The crow lost no time and dived in. But alas! When he emerged, he saw that he was dark in colour. He seethed with anger and cawed at the owl, "Why have you made me black? Wait till I catch you!" The frightened owl flew away and came out only at night when the crow was asleep. Since then, crows are black and owls' venture out only at night.

21 The Trickster Monkey

There lived a very naughty monkey named Mogri who loved to play pranks on other animals. He would drop rotten fruits on other animals and laugh at their discomfort. Samba the lion didn't find Mogri's tricks funny. It was insulting for the king of the jungle to have rotten fruits flung at him. He warned Mogri, "Wait! I'll teach you a lesson soon." But Mogri was too quick and managed to escape each time.

One day, Mogri dropped an overripe mango on Samba's nose. But unfortunately, the branch on which he was sitting broke and he fell right on the lion's back. Samba roared in anger and twisted from side to side to shake Mogri off. But the monkey clung tightly onto the lion's back. Samba charged through the forest, yet Mogri, though terrified, remained on his back.

Finally tired, Samba bent down to drink water from a pond. Mogri took this opportunity to make good his escape. Ever since, Mogri was too terrified to play a trick on Samba.

22 The Fox with a Snapped Tail

Once, Kallu the fox, was wandering in the forest when his tail got stuck in a snare. He pulled at it so hard that the tail snapped and a part of it remained in the trap. Kallu was very sad and envied the other foxes who had bushy tails.

He said to the other foxes, "You know friends, these tails are useless extensions to our bodies. They feel very odd and they look so bad! I suggest you cut them off! Look how freely I walk about!"

The other foxes saw through his jealousy and told Kallu, "If you are so free and feel good without your full tail, then why are you looking so unhappy without one?" Kallu quickly left the place in shame.

23 The Rabbit Goes Duck Hunting

Once upon a time, there was a very boastful rabbit. He claimed that he knew and could perform every task. He would often fool people to prove his worth. One day, he met an otter on his way to catch ducks and claimed that he could catch ducks as well. The otter was not surprised because he knew that the rabbit was lying. The otter quickly went to the river and began his search. The rabbit in the meantime gathered a pole and tied a noose to it, thinking that ducks get caught that way. He dived into the water with it and waited for the ducks to arrive. Suddenly, out flew a duck with the pole and the rabbit hanging from the noose. The duck shook the pole vigorously, forcing the rabbit to jump on the ground. The otter popped his head out and started laughing at the rabbit saying, "So that's how you catch ducks!" The rabbit scampered away with broken limbs and was never heard boasting again.

24 Shelley the Flying Turtle

On a bright sunny morning, Shelley and her turtle siblings popped out of broken eggs. Suddenly, they noticed a flock of seagulls swooping down. The seagulls cawed and squeaked and picked up all the turtles one by one and flew away. Shelley cried as she noticed her siblings being taken away. A crab, who heard Shelley's loud wails, came out of his cave and asked, "Are you crying because the seagulls carried away your siblings?" "Yes," answered Shelley. "Every year millions of baby turtles are eaten up by seagulls," said the crab wiping Shelley's tears. He took her to his cave. There, he introduced her to his friends, Barney the barnacle, Slouch the sea slug and Buff the mussel. "We are all scared of seagulls because they either eat us or peck us to death," said the animals. Next morning, when Shelley and her friends went to the beach, a seagull attacked Shelley. Shelley ran as fast as she could and suddenly flapped her flippers and found herself flying. "I can fly!" she screamed. Her friends were startled to see a turtle flying. Since then, Shelley became unafraid because whenever the seagulls swooped down, she flew away. After a few years, when Shelley gave birth to baby turtles, she kept a close watch on them and as soon as the seagulls neared them, Shelley ordered her babies to climb on her back and flapping her flippers, flew away!

25 Dancing Monkeys

Once, a prince had twelve monkeys. They were very good dancers. They would wear make-up and bright costumes and dance. All those who watched the monkeys' dance, thought that they were humans. Word spread far and wide about their performance and people from all over flocked to see them perform. One day, a courtier decided to play a trick on the dancing monkeys. When the monkeys began to dance, the courtier took out a handful of peanuts and hurled them on the dance floor. As soon as the monkeys saw the nuts, they forgot all about dancing and leapt to grab the peanuts. They pulled off their masks and tore their robes and fought with each other. Now, the reality came out. People cried out in surprise, "Look! These are monkeys!" The prince realised that monkeys will remain monkeys even though they dressed like humans.

26 A Cartload of Almonds

Once, a squirrel used to work for a lion. He was a dedicated worker and finished all his tasks on time. All his friends enjoyed themselves while working, but the squirrel refused to leave because the lion had promised him a cartload of almonds. Now squirrels love almonds and rarely get a chance to eat them. The squirrel worked even harder to impress the lion with his work. Years passed and it was time for the squirrel to retire from service. The lion was a good master and he organised a grand farewell for his dedicated servant. As promised, the cartload of almonds was also presented to him. The squirrel accepted it graciously. He went home to enjoy his treat, but alas! Now he was too old and had lost all his teeth!

27 The Fox and the Lion

Once, there lived a fox who wanted to make friends with the lion even though he was frightened of him. The other animals tried to warn him about the danger in befriending such a ferocious animal but he didn't care. "I'll show you that the lion is not so dangerous after all," he declared. So, the next time the lion passed his way, the fox approached the lion a little closer than before. This time, the fox did not feel as frightened as earlier. The third time the fox came even closer to the lion and even talked with him, asking him about his welfare. "King Lion, I hope to see you again soon," said the fox and shaking his tail, slipped away from there. His fear of the lion had almost gone. He was happy to have overcome his fear at last.

28 The Lion and the Hare

Once a hungry lion, while searching for food in the jungle found a hare sleeping peacefully under a tree. "Oh! That's a lovely fluffy hare. It will surely make a great meal," he thought smacking his lips. Just as he was going to grab the animal, he saw a zebra passing by. The hungry lion thought, "Why not eat the zebra first and then return to the hare!" As soon as the alert zebra saw the lion, he quickly frisked away. Dissapointed for having lost such a great catch, the lion returned only to find that the hare had left too! He said, "How foolish I was! I let go what I already had in hand in the hope of obtaining more."

29 The Lion, the Fox and the Beasts

One day, an old, sick lion invited all the animals to his den. He announced that he would read out his last will. One by one, many animals—the horse, the goat, the monkey and the zebra, entered the lion's den. After some time, however, the animals stopped coming. The worried lion came out and found a fox waiting outside. "Why isn't any one else coming inside?" he enquired. The wise fox said, "My Lord, we noticed that all the footmarks led to your den but none had come out." The angry lion growled loudly while the animals fled away. The wise fox went to the other animals and said, "Now you know why I say, it is easy to get into an enemy's web but difficult to emerge safe."

30 How the Ewe Outwitted the Jackal

Once, a jackal and an ewe agreed to work together in a farm. When the crop was harvested, the jackal took four shares of the harvest but gave the ewe only one share despite her hard work. "I think this should be enough for you," said the cunning jackal.

The ewe felt cheated and went to the dog and told him about the jackal's unfair behaviour. The dog promised to help the ewe. He hid inside a wicker basket. When the ewe and the jackal met on the farm, the ewe said to the jackal, "Brother, could you lift my little lambs from there?" pointing to the basket.

The jackal was very pleased thinking of the tasty meal the lambs would make and rushed to open the basket. But as soon as he saw the dog's sharp teeth, he let out a yell and ran leaving all the grain.

Contents

The Story of the Month: The Four Friends

The Story of the Month

The Four Friends

01 The Four Friends

Once upon a time in a jungle lived four friends—Chitranga the deer, Mandharaka the turtle, Laghupatanka the crow and Hiranyaka the mouse. All of them used to gather around the river and exchange stories of their past experiences of life. They would often sit near the river. Mandharaka would catch fish for his friends while Chitranga would chew green grass from nearby fields.

One day Mandharaka, Laghupatanka and Hiranyaka as usual gathered near the river to spend time together. They waited for Chitranga, but even after a few hours there was no sign of Chitranga. Mandharaka got worried, "I hope everything is fine with our friend. It is very unusual of our friend not to be here by this time." "Do not worry, he must have gone to the far end of the forest to meet his other friends," replied Hiranyaka. Afternoon waned off and still Chitranga did not come. The three friends were really worried now because the deer always told them if he had to go far. Hiranyaka said, "Laghupatanka, can you fly around and check if our friend is in any trouble? I feel he is somewhere trapped in a hunter's net." Laghupatanka flew away. He crossed the river and flew towards the field where the deer went for grazing. There in the open space, he saw his dear friend trapped under the hunter's

net. Laghupatanka landed near his friend. Chitranga's sad face lit up and tears of joy streamed down his cheeks, "Oh! I am so happy to see you. Please save me from this trap." Laghupatanka lost no time. He flew back and narrated everything to his friends. All three of them sat and planned how they could rescue their friend.

It was decided that Hiranyaka would fly on Laghupatanka's back and cut the net with his sharp teeth. Soon Chitranga was free and all friends were again happy. As they were rejoicing, the hunter approached. He was angry seeing his net shredded and the deer missing.

All friends ran as fast as they could. But poor Mandharaka could not escape. The hunter saw him and captured him in his bag. Laghupatanka shouted, "We must save our friend." They decided that Chitranga would deliberately come in the hunter's path to distract his attention. Meanwhile, Laghupatanka would fly away with the bag and Hiranyaka would cut its strings. As per the plan when the hunter saw the beautiful deer, he was overjoyed and ran after the animal leaving the bag. The crow picked up the unguarded bag and flew away. Chitranga too ran very fast and was out of the hunter's reach. The hunter soon came back to get his bag but that too was gone. He mourned, "My greediness has undone me." Disappointed, he went back empty-handed. Hiranyaka cut open the strings of the bag and Mandharaka was free. All of them were happy and agreed that they were lucky to have such helpful friends. Once again all the friends were together by the riverside.

02 One Good Turn Deserves Another

Once there lived a forgetful squirrel named Cyril who loved nuts. He would collect nuts the whole day but at the end of the day, he would forget where he had kept them. One day, seeing him so puzzled, the glow worms asked, "What happened, friend?" Cyril told them his problem. They promised that, henceforth, they would glow at that place where he would keep his nuts.

Cyril was a good-hearted squirrel. He wanted to help the glow worms in return for their help. "My mother says a good turn deserves another. So tell me how can I help you?" he asked. The glow worms were happy. They said, "Cyril, if you could make the ground smooth with your bushy tail it would help us."

The next morning, Cyril woke up but he had forgotten what was to be done. He dug the ground with his paws making it bumpier. The glow worms knew Cyril was good-hearted but just forgetful by nature, so they still kept on marking the hideouts for him.

03 The Nice Fox

Murphy was an honest and friendly fox. He felt very sad whenever others said that they did not trust a fox. "Why does everyone mistrust the Fox family? I will prove all of them wrong," he thought. He went towards Farmer Fred's farm. He reached the chicken coop and called out, "Hello friends, I am a good fox and am here to help you." The chickens found it hard to believe and replied, "A fox wants to help us! We don't believe you." As they were thus talking, Farmer Fred saw Murphy and let his dogs after him.

Murphy ran as fast as he could. He reached his den with a heavy heart. He sat down in front of his den, feeling sad and lonely. Suddenly he heard a boy say, "Look what a beautiful fox it is! I am going to take his photograph." Murphy posed happily for his picture and felt that at least there were some who appreciated him.

04   The Hawk and the Hen

Once upon a time a hawk fell in love with a hen. "Will you marry me?" he asked her. The hen was happy to agree. The hawk gave her a ring. Now, the hen had also agreed to marry a cock. When the cock saw her wearing the ring, he was angry. "I will kill you if you marry that hawk!" he shouted.

Frightened, the hen immediately removed the ring and threw it away. After a few days, when the hawk came to see his beloved, he saw that she was not wearing his ring. "Where is the ring?" he asked. She said, "A snake snatched it from me! I am still looking for it…"

But the hawk knew that the hen was lying. He cursed her saying, "As a punishment for your deception, you shall keep scratching this earth till you find the ring."

Since that day, hens have the habit of scratching the ground!

05   The Horse and the Ass

Long, long ago, an ass lived in a small town in London. He worked for a man who always loaded him with bricks. One day, the ass was carrying bricks uphill, when he met a horse passing by. The horse walked elegantly in its finest trappings and he had no load on him. The surprised ass remarked, "How lucky you are! You do not have to carry load like me. Instead you are dressed in the finest of trappings." The horse didn't reply but went his way. Next day, the ass was ordered to carry bundles of food sacks to the battleground. As he was walking past the wounded soldiers, he came across the same horse he had met the day before. The horse was badly wounded. Now the ass understood what the horse's job was. The ass thought, "I was wrong. It is better to have humble security than gilded danger."

06 Susie Swallow

Susie was a chirpy little swallow. The whole day long she would fly around moving from one tree to another. Whenever, she was tired, she would sit on a treetop and rest for a while. One day while sitting on a tall tree, she noticed that the colour of the leaves had changed from dark green to pale green. Susie wondered whether the tree was ill. Next day when she came to the tree, she found that the colour of the leaves had turned brown. "Oh! The leaves are dying. All its leaves are falling off. Now the tree will feel cold," she thought. She flew hurriedly to her mother and asked, "Mama, why are all the leaves of the tree falling off?" Mama Swallow patted her feathers and said, "Susie, the tree is not dying. The falling leaves are the sign of the autumn season. Soon we will have winter in this place… Come, we will fly away to a place where the sun shines through out the day and it is warm." And Mama Swallow and Susie flew away with the pack of swallows to warmer lands.

07 The Crocodile's Tail

A very hungry crocodile was lying in wait for animals to come to the river. "No animal has come today to the river. I will soon die of hunger." In the same river, lived a crab who sympathised with the crocodile and agreed to help him in searching food "Thanks, Crab! Would you bring the jackal near the river? We will share the meat," asked the crocodile. So the crab went into the forest to bring a jackal to the crocodile. He found the jackal eating a fowl. "Oh, after this hearty meal, you must be thirsty. Come, I will take you to the river," called out the crab. The jackal was clever and replied, "Thank you, but I am not thirsty." Unseen, he tiptoed behind the crab. When the crocodile heard this, he was furious. Now they decided the crab would go to the jackal and give him the news of the crocodile's death. The next day, hearing the crab, the jackal went to the riverside and said aloud, "I know the crocodile is not dead because even when crocodiles are dead, their tails move." The crocodile at once started wagging his tail. The jackal laughed aloud, "You fool! I was just testing you," and fled to safety.

08 Pirate Pig

Alan the pig loved to read about pirates and their treasure hunts. Alan lived near a pond, which had many friendly ducks. There was a tiny island in the middle of the pond. Alan thought, "If I get to that island, I can hunt treasure like the pirates!" He found a tub floating about in the pond and got into it. He made a black flag and drew a scary skull and two crossbones on it. Then he got an eye patch and a tiny knife. After Alan reached the island, he searched for the treasure all day but did not find any. In the evening, when Alan wanted to go back, he found the tub missing. He looked for it everywhere and suddenly remembered that he had forgotten to tie his boat up and it must have floated away. Alan sat crying by the shore. Just then, a friendly duck who saw Alan crying, brought the tub back to Alan. Alan was safe but he never ever wanted to become a pirate pig again!

09 The Hippo That Skied

Hilda was not at all like the other hippos. All day, her family would wallow in the muddy pool but she would stand in the rain and enjoy the water trickling down her skin. "Come, Hilda. This mud is warm like chocolate," her brother would call. But Hilda did not go. Her favourite pastime was trying to float on the big lotus leaves in the pond, but alas! She would always sink down like a stone. But Hilda never gave up trying.

In the pond lived her friends, the two frogs. They helped her and after lots of hard practice, Hilda finally learnt to float. "Hey look! I am floating!" she shouted one day. A photographer saw her. He said, "Why don't you come to my country? There are snow-covered mountains, you would love it." Hilda flew with him in an aeroplane. The people loved Hilda and came to watch her skiing. They even awarded her a gold medal. When Hilda returned to her pond, she showed her gold medal to her frog friends. "Hilda is a famous hippo!" said everyone.

10 The Frogs and the Well

Once upon a time there was a big marshy forest where there was plenty of rainfall. However, one year there was no rain. All the marsh and swamps began to dry up. The animals were worried and started moving to different places. In the river lived two frogs. They too were worried. One said, "Oh friend, what do we do now? The water has dried up and there are no snails left to eat." The other one said, "Let's go before it is too late for us."

The two of them started on their search for water. After a long day's hopping, they arrived at a deep well. The first one was happy. Peeping inside he croaked, "Let us jump inside." The second was wiser, "Wait!" he said. He picked up a stone and hurled it into the water. The stone cracked against the dry floor of the well. "You must always first look before you leap," he advised his friend.

11 The Wolf in Sheep's Clothing

Once there lived a wicked wolf. "All animals ran away from me. How am I suppose to get food?" thought the wolf. "I must disguise myself," he decided. The next day, he covered himself in a sheep's cloak. He went to the nearby pastures where a flock of sheep were grazing and mingled among them. He was happy that so far, even the shepherd hadn't been able to see through his false skin. "Ah! Tonight I will finally get sheep's meat," chuckled the wolf. Night came and the shepherd locked them all in the sheep's pen. As the wolf was about to remove his skin, the shepherd came to get meat for himself and unknowingly took away the wolf.

12 The Turtle and the Lizard

Tommy the turtle and Lily the lizard were two friends. One day, they went to steal ginger from a house. But the owner of the house chased the animals away with a stick. The quick Lily ran fast to a safe place, leaving the slow Tommy behind. Tommy hurriedly hid himself under a coconut shell. He was sad that his friend didn't come to his help. The next day, Tommy the turtle showed Lily the lizard a honeycomb. And once again the lizard ran faster than his friend to grab the first bite. But alas! The lizard was stung by the angry bees! Tommy realised just how greedy his friend was. He thought of a plan to teach the lizard a lesson. He took him to a trap and said, "This is a silver necklace that my grandfather gifted me." The lizard pushed Tommy to grab it, but was trapped instead.

13 The Lion and the Boar

One hot summer afternoon a lion and a boar went in search of water. After a long search, they came to a watering hole. The water looked refreshing. The lion wanted to drink from the watering hole first and so did the boar. They started to argue and soon, both the animals started to fight. Soon the quarrel turned into a violent fight. Though both were severely wounded, they continued fighting. After some time, the animals stopped to catch their breath. That is when they heard two vultures talking, "Let us wait for a little while more. Both these animals will kill each other in this fight. Then we can eat them up!" The lion and the boar realised how useless their fight was. They at once made up saying, "It is better for us to become friends rather than be eaten up by vultures."

14 Percy and Polly

Once upon a time two mice, Percy and Polly, lived in the attic of an old house. One day, a hungry Polly said to her friend, "Percy, let us go and hunt for cheese." They saw a big block of cheese lying on a wooden board in the kitchen. Polly was overjoyed. As she was about to grab it, Percy stopped her midway, "It is a mouse trap! Let us move out quickly. Cousin Matilda, who lives in the garden, always wants us to stay with her."

The next night, Percy and Polly noiselessly slipped out of the attic and headed towards the garden. While they were squeezing themselves out of the back door into the fresh air of the garden, Percy saw an owl overhead and yelled, "Polly, hide! The owl will catch us." Polly hid behind the big bushes. She was very thankful to her friend for saving her life. From that day onwards, all three of them lived happily in the garden ever after, but they always kept a watchful eye out for the owl.

15 Meeku's Long Tail

Once there lived a mouse named Meeku, who had a very long tail. At school, all his friends made fun of him. "Look at that funny tail," they would mock. Meeku felt very sad. One day, while returning home, he found his class-mate, Chinu, crying loudly near a tree. On asking Chinu, the latter explained how Tomu, the tom cat had snatched his delicious sandwiches. "I'll definitely get the sand-wiches," Meeku assured Chinu. Then Meeku saw Tomu digging out earth to hide the sandwiches there. Meeku quickly hid behind a tree. He heard Tomu saying, "Let me wrap the sandwiches in a cloth and tie them to this long root and hide it in the bush." The long root was actually Meeku's tail! Tomu carefully tied the sandwiches to the tail. As soon as the cat was gone, Meeku ran with the sandwiches and gave it to Chinu. At school, Chinu told everybody about Meeku's bravery. Since then, Meeku was no longer jeered at for his long tail.

16   It's Only Lorna!

Once there lived three friends, Duffy, Fiffy and Taffy, in a grassy valley. Duffy was a huge brown bear, Fiffy, a striped raccoon and Taffy, a brown little squirrel. They spent their days playing without any worry as there were no wild animals to scare them. One day, the three friends were playing hide and seek. It was Taffy's turn to count while Duffy and Taffy scurried off to hide. Duffy hid behind a brown-coloured boulder while Fiffy hid amidst a bush. When Taffy finished counting, he looked all over the valley and called out to Duffy, "Come out, Duffy! You are so huge and furry that I can easily see you!" Soon, they both found Fiffy too. Just then, they heard a huge roar. The three friends were frightened. "Who could that be? There are no lions or tigers in this valley!" cried Taffy. Just then, they saw their friend Lorna the cow. "You are a cow! Why are you roaring like this?"they cried. She giggled and said that she was only trying to trick them. All the four friends laughed and continued their game of hide and seek.

17   The Falcon and the Duck

One day, Papa Duck said to his family, "Dear ones, it is getting very cold here. Let us all fly off to a warmer place." All of them agreed with him. Mama Duck led the ducklings, while Papa Duck flew at the end. As they were flying over the ocean, a falcon started following them. Mama Duck warned them, "Danger! Danger!" And all ducks scattered. The falcon attacked Papa Duck, who was at the end of the line, but he flew very fast and was saved. A few months passed by and the duck family was now flying back through the same route. This time, Papa Duck bragged, "Children, it was here that I defeated the falcon!" The falcon was nearby when he heard this. He was angry and thought, "This time you will not escape me!" And he flew with great speed and had a great fight with Papa Duck. So one should not brag about oneself, especially in the enemy's territory.

18 Ossie's Umbrella

Ossie was a happy ostrich. She only had one regret—she could not fly. "Why do I have so many feathers when I cannot fly?" she would mutter to herself. "Maybe, if I run fast and take off, then I may fly up into the air." So she would always run fast hoping that one day she would fly high up in the air.

Once, while running, she came across a beautiful snake, "Oh, you poor thing! You are lying on the ground. Can't you run?" Ossie teased the snake. The snake didn't reply and Ossie was ashamed that she had hurt the snake. "I am sorry," she apologised. Ober the rhino was watching her. He laughed aloud, "You silly creature, this is not a snake. It is an umbrella." Ossie opened the umbrella. Just then a strong breeze lifted Ossie up in the air. Ossie was delighted. "Wheeeeee! I can fly! I will always keep this umbrella with me and whenever there is strong breeze, I will open it up and fly."

19 The Wolf Who Turned Good

Once upon a time there lived a wicked wolf. He prowled around the city to prey on people and animals. Everybody was frightened of him. One day, while wandering in the forest, he met a stranger who looked like an angel. The wolf felt a strange feeling overcoming him. He knelt down with his head lowered in front of the man. The man said, "Oh Wolf! Why do you harm others? If you spread hatred, others will hate you too. Promise me that you'll be good to others and not hurt anyone." The wolf promised him and when he looked up he found that the man had gone. Since that day, the wolf became a good animal. He stopped attacking people and animals. In return, the people of the city gave him food to eat and looked after him.

20 The Friendly Bird

A farmer was walking across the field when he saw an injured bird. He picked it up and took it home. "You foolish man! We hardly have enough to eat and you have brought another mouth to feed," said his wife angrily. Everyday, the farmer would feed the bird with grains and tend to its injuries. Soon the bird recovered. One day, the farmer came home and saw the bird had flown away. The heartbroken farmer went in search of the bird.

Soon he came to the bird's colony. The bird was happy to see him. The other birds thanked him for nursing their friend and as a to-ken of their love, gave him a box. The farmer took the box to his wife. When she opened the box, she found wonderful jewels inside. She was very happy and no longer scolded him for tending to the bird.

21 The Fox and the Crow

A fox was walking past a jungle. He saw a crow perched on a tree with a juicy piece of cheese. The fox's mouth watered. His stomach growled in hunger and he desperately wanted to eat the cheese. He quickly thought of a way in which he could trick the crow. He went up to the crow and said, "You are such a handsome and clever bird! If only you could sing just as beautifully!"

The foolish crow puffed up his feathers at the praise. He wanted to prove to the fox that he could sing very well too. "Caw, caw!" he opened his mouth to sing. Plop! The juicy piece of cheese fell to the ground. The wily fox was waiting for just this opportunity. He gobbled the cheese and went his way.

22 Battle of the Crabs

Once upon a time, some crabs lived along the shore of a sea. They were quite disturbed by the noisy waves and so couldn't sleep easily. The bigger crabs decided to do something about it. "Let us fight these waves!" said one of them.

A shrimp saw the crabs who gathered at the shore. "What are you doing, friends?" asked the shrimp. "We are going to fight the waves!" replied the crabs. The shrimp laughed at them and said, "Ha! Ha! How will you fight these huge waves with your tiny bodies?"

The shrimp pointed to the spear on his head and said, "This is my weapon that will shield me from the waves!" The foolish crabs believed him and praised the shrimp for his courage. They begged the shrimp to lead their army. Just then, a huge wave came rushing in and killed all of them. Till today, you can find crabs running towards the waves to fight it, but when their courage fails they hurry back to the shore.

23 The Monkey's Mess

"Yeouch!" cried Kallu the monkey. A thorn pierced through his paw. He went to a barber to get the thorn out. But while removing the thorn with a razor, the barber cut off Kallu's tail by mistake. The angry monkey said, "Attach back my tail or give me your razor!" The poor barber gave him his razor.

On his way back home, Kallu saw a woman cutting wood. Kallu gave her the razor. The woman happily used the razor, but it broke while cutting wood. Angry Kallu said, "Fix my razor or give me your wood!" So, Kallu took her wood and went away. He met a man baking cakes and gave him the wood. The man happily burnt Kallu's wood. Now, Kallu demanded, "Give me back my wood, or give me your cakes!" Just when Kallu was about to eat the cakes, a dog came running and snatched the cakes away from him.

24 The Dawn Chorus

Everyday before the sun arose, 'The Dawn Chorus' consisting of the black bird, the finch and the rooster sang tuneful songs to wake up the world. The black bird was the leader of the band and one day became very angry at the finch for reaching late. "How can we wake up people if you reach late?" he asked the finch. The finch was very upset for he always overslept. The wise owl, who was the finch's neighbour, asked him, "Why are you looking so worried, Mr. Finch?" The finch explained to him his problem. "I have a solution," said the owl nodding his head wisely. "Since I am on duty every night and come home at the wee hours, I will wake you up just before going to bed." The finch was elated and thanked the owl for his support. Since then, the finch always joined 'The Dawn Chorus' on time and they all sang melodious songs to wake up the world.

25 The Foolish Donkey

Once, a naughty donkey found a lion's skin. He put on the skin and tried to imitate a lion. He went on scaring the other little animals around. The donkey thought, "Now everyone thinks I am a lion! Look at how they run away!"

While the other animals ran helter-skelter, a fox happened to pass by. The clever fox did not get scared. So, the donkey tried to scare him by roaring like a lion! But how can a donkey roar? It can only bray! Just then, all the animals realised their folly and gave the naughty donkey a sound thrashing.

The fox laughed and said, "You are such a dumb donkey! Don't you know that donkeys can't roar?" The donkey hung his head in shame when he realised how foolish he was.

26 Professor Fox

Once upon a time, there lived a Mama Tortoise with her three infants in a shady spot by the river. One day, a fox, who lived in the nearby forest, saw the baby tortoises and started making plans of how he could make a tasty meal of them up. "They look all plump and delicious!" cried the fox smacking his lips. One morning, when the fox went to drink water from the river, he saw Mama Tortoise. He immediately greeted the tortoise, "Friend, I don't see you these days," said the fox warmly. "Oh! I've been busy with my little children," said Mama Tortoise.

"Oh yes, your children must be growing fast now. Why don't you send them to my school? I'll sing them some melodious songs and also teach them how to be good tortoises," suggested the clever fox. Mama Tortoise was very pleased by the fox's suggestion. The next morning she happily led her children to the fox's hole. That night, the fox ate up one of them. After two days, Mama Tortoise went to see her kids. The fox showed her the two children and said that the third one had been sent to his brother, who was a higher scholar and a great musician. That night, the fox ate up the remaining two baby tortoises. A crow informed Mama Tortoise about what had happened to her kids. Overcome with anger and grief, the tortoise swore to take revenge. The next day when she met the fox near the river, she greeted him, pretending to be unaware of what had happened. "Brother Fox, would you like to take a ride on my back to the other side of the river?" she asked. "Oh! That would be great," said the fox and hopped onto her back. Halfway through the river, the tortoise sank deep into the river and drowned the fox. "You villain! This is what you deserve for what you did to my innocent children," said Mama Tortoise.

27 Minky and Richard

Once upon a time there lived a tiny mouse called Minky and a mighty lion called Richard. One day, Minky was passing by Richard's den. Richard pounced upon poor little Minky and was about to gobble him when the little mouse pleaded, "Sir, please let me go! I promise you that I will do you a good turn one day, if you do not eat me!" Richard found this really funny and roared loudly, "What can you do for me, Minky? Anyways, I will let you go for now!"

Two weeks later, some huntsmen came to the forest and spread a net around Richard's den and trapped him. Little Minky was hunting for food when he heard Richard roaring. He ran to him. Seeing the lion caught in the net, Minky started gnawing at it with his sharp teeth and he soon freed Richard. From that day onwards, Minky and Richard were the best of friends.

28 A Home for Two Cats

Once upon a time, there was a black cat called Boris. He lived with other cats in an animal shelter. All of them made fun of Boris. "You are black," said one. "You bring ill luck!" cried one of the cats. "People are scared of you," mocked another cat. Boris lowered his face and cried. "Nobody likes me," he thought. Just then, his only friend in the shelter, Taffy, a Persian cat, came along. "Don't pay attention to such bitter comments and pray to God!" said Taffy. "Who is God?" asked Boris. "God is like a father. He has created you and me and the whole universe" explained Taffy. "Why should I pray to God?" asked Boris. "He is very kind and helpful. If you pray to Him, He shall fulfill all your dreams," replied Taffy. Boris closed his eyes and prayed to God, "Oh God, please find a home for Taffy and me." The next day, an old lady visited the shelter. She liked both Boris and Taffy and took them home.

29 The Crow

Once, a holy princess was sleeping when an injured crow flew into her room and cried for help. "Who has hurt you like this?" asked the concerned princess. "I am a prince and a wicked witch, who lives in my castle, has transformed me into a crow. She says that only a good natured princess can release me from this spell. I searched everywhere, but couldn't find one. Will you please help me?" asked the crow. The princess immediately agreed to help and went with the crow to his castle. The crow said, "At night you shall see ghosts roaming in this room, but if you scream, I will not be released from the spell." When it was night and the princess was alone, ugly ghosts crowded her room and tried to scare her. But, the princess did not get scared and seeing the brave princess, the evil ghosts disappeared. The crow changed into a handsome prince and married the princess and they lived happily ever after.

30 The Monster in the Moon

Once upon a time, two little squirrels lived on the branch of a tree. One night, when they were watching the moon through their telescope, they saw a dark figure in it. "Is it a monster?" they wondered. "Its eyes shine so bright," said one of them. The two little squirrels scampered along to ask their father about it. "What is that dark figure we see in the moon, Father? Is it a monster that wakes up every night?" asked one of them. Their father became curious too and watched through a telescope. Instead, he found Ollie the owl sitting on the branch of a tree. "Ha! Ha! Ha!" he laughed and said, "That's Ollie, the owl whose figure you see every night against the moon. Actually, owls have big bulging eyes, which sparkle in the dark. You must have been scared seeing that." The young squirrels were relieved to know that it was just an owl and not a monster.

31 The Animal Olympics

Long ago, all the animals of various forests used to wait for the animal Olympics, a major sporting event that used to take place in the forest. Like always, this year too, all the animals had gathered and were really excited about their performances. Everybody was busy practising. Monkeys, the pole vault champions, practised leaping high above the pole, while the elephants practised throwing the javelin miles away with their trunks. Meanwhile, Mr. Lion, the President of the Olympics Committee, looked into the preparations. The fields were cleared, tracks laid and flags hung. The day of the events finally arrived. While the lion was inspecting the field, he saw the tortoise standing at a distance and crying. "Why are you so upset?" he enquired. "Sir, as I am very slow, I can never win in any event no matter how hard I try," explained the sad tortoise. "That doesn't matter. We need a person to fire the pistol at the starting line and you can do that," said the lion. The tortoise was very happy.

After a while, the lion came across the cheetah, standing with a glum face. "Now, why are you so sad?" asked the concerned lion "Sir, I am the fastest animal on the earth. If I participate in any event, I will easily win. But, then there will be no fun left in the contest," he sobbed. "No problem, for we have the perfect job for you. You can carry the Olympic torch," said the Lion. That day all the animals had great fun watching the games, but the tortoise and the cheetah were the happiest.

Contents

The Story of the Month: The Proud Rabbit and the Moon

November

The Proud Rabbit and the Moon

01 The Proud Rabbit and the Moon

Snowy was a very proud bunny rabbit. He had long pink ears, a bushy tail and soft white fur. He was also quite wise, which is why everyone admired him. But he was very vain. "I'm not only handsome but learned too," Snowy would often boast to his friends. Snowy was so full of himself that many animals did not like his company and avoided him. But there were a few young rabbits who wanted to be like Snowy. This made Snowy feel like a hero and he became prouder and prouder.

One night, Snowy was lying on a carpet of thick grass and reading a book in the moonlight. Suddenly, his eyes fell on the surface of the moon and he spoke aloud, "Ptshh… how dirty the moon looks with all her black marks. But this book I'm reading praises the moon. How funny!"

The moon heard Snowy's remarks and angrily said, "Oh! What a foolish rabbit you are! Everyone praises me because I light up the whole world at night. If it were not for me, the world would be in total darkness." "Ha! Ha! Ha!" laughed Snowy.

At this, the moon lost her temper and said, "Wait and watch what happens if I am not around," and disappeared behind the clouds. All of a sudden it became very dark. Snowy could hardly see anything. He couldn't even see the way to his burrow. "Grrrr…" Snowy heard the tiger growling nearby. Clat! Clat! Clat! His teeth trembled in fear hearing the weird noises. "I can hardly see anything around and the tiger seems to be very near. What shall I do now?" Suddenly he remembered his mother's old friend, Aunt Owl who lived just on the tree near the hedges. "I better seek Aunt Owl's help," thought Snowy and yelled out, "Aunt Owl, please help me find my burrow. I can't see anything in the dark and a tiger is around. Pray save me."

"Screech…" came a sound and then popped out Aunt Owl from her hole in the tree. She saw Snowy crying for help. But suddenly she remembered how Snowy often made fun of her ugly looks and her voice. She had even overheard him challenging the moon. Filled with disgust, Aunt Owl decided not to help Snowy find his burrow so that the arrogant rabbit would learn a lesson. Knowing fully well that the tiger might pounce on him any moment, Aunt Owl flew away saying, "This serves you right. You often make fun of me and do not respect me. Why should I help you? You can help yourself." Helpless Snowy kept leaping in the dark trying to find his way. He could sense that the tiger was waiting to pounce on him. He begged Aunt Owl to help him and promised to mend his ways. Aunt Owl was kind and agreed to save him. She flew in front of the tiger's eyes to distract him while Snowy dashed away to hide in the bushes. He had learnt his lesson today.

02   Mr. Hawk and Brer Rabbit

One day Brer Rabbit was roaming about in the forest. He plucked the wild berries and fruits that grew along the way. Suddenly, he noticed a shadow following him. He looked up and saw a hawk circling above him. The hawk swooped down and grabbed him. Brer Rabbit struggled and begged the hawk to let him go. Then he tried hard to free himself, but all in vain. "Oh! Uncle Hawk, why do you want to kill a harmless creature like me? I'm too small for you," cried Brer Rabbit. "Brer Rabbit, I'm not going to let you go," said the hawk. Just then, an idea struck Brer Rabbit and he said to the hawk, "Uncle Hawk, first you must tame me. Right now I'm wild, so I won't taste so good. When I grow up, I'll run into the bushes and grab partridges for you. And when I become fat, I'll taste even better," added the crafty rabbit.

The hawk thought that the rabbit was talking sense and while he was wondering what to do, his grip over Brer Rabbit loosened. The rabbit wriggled free and fled So the Hawk was never able to catch and eat either Brer Rabbit or the partridges!

03   The Hungry Little Dog

Once there was a hungry little dog called Maxi. He would wander the whole day in search of food and sleep under the street lamp at night. Sometimes, people would throw a slice of bread or dog biscuits at him. At times, Maxi would be very excited and run into people's lawns and bark loudly knocking into whatever came his way. They thought he was mad but Maxi was actually a very special dog.

One day, a stout gentleman watched Maxi prancing about on the street and barking in excitement. Suddenly, the gentleman jumped with delight and exclaimed, "At last I've found the right dog for my films!" Knowing that Maxi was hungry, the kind film director got some meat from the butchers for Maxi and then took him home. Soon, Maxi started performing antics on films that thrilled all. He made his master rich! Maxi had become a film star.

04 The Sick Wolf and the Sheep

Once upon a time, a wolf who lived near Mr. Peter's farm, escaped from a pack of wild hounds. After running for a while he felt really hungry. He looked around for some time and then saw a little sheep grazing in the meadow. The wolf's mouth watered at the sight of the sheep and he thought, "Ah! At last I have something to eat." He said to the sheep politely, "Little sheep, little sheep! I'm very ill. Can you get me some water to drink? Then maybe I will get the energy to find something to eat. I'll be so grateful to you." The sheep was clever. He understood that the wolf was trying to trap him. He replied, "If I obey your order, I'll be risking my own life. You will make a meal of me." And as he said this, he bounced away from the wolf.

05 Jaunty the Kangaroo

Jaunty the kangaroo felt out of place in the company of other animals in the zoo. While the other animals amused the children visiting the zoo, Jaunty could not do anything funny. One day, Mr. Robert, the owner of the zoo, came to Jaunty and told him that he would not be allowed to live in the zoo unless he entertained the children. He said, "Why don't you give them a ride?" At this, the kangaroo said, "How can I do that? They will all slide off my back." Soon, an idea struck Mr. Robert and he ordered Jaunty to carry the children in his pouch. All the little children lined up to get into the kangaroo's pouch. The children's joy knew no bounds, for the tiny tots felt like they were flying when the kangaroo hopped around. It was like a roller coaster ride! From that day onwards, Jaunty lived happily with the other animals of the zoo.

06 Flying Field Mice

Jim and Tim were two field mice. One day in the farm, they were sitting and looking up at the bright blue sky. Suddenly, Tim spotted something moving in the sky. It was a helicopter. "Oh! I wish we could fly," he said. Then Jim exclaimed in wonder, "Someone just jumped out." Tim and Jim watched with disbelief. A parachute landed on the ground and a man gently emerged from it. "How nice to go flying and parachuting," said Jim. "But we're too small!" sighed Tim. All at once, Jim hopped to the top of a maple tree. "Hey Tim, look up, see where I am." And as he said this, he jumped into the air. Tim also joined him and they both had a great time hopping and jumping up and down on the maple tree.

07 The Donkey's Ears

Long ago, when God was creating animals, He decided to make the donkey. After He had finished, He proudly announced, "Henceforth, dear creature, you shall be called a donkey!" "Thank you!" said the donkey meekly and went to join the other animals on the Earth.

He walked a few steps and then stood still and thought, "Oh, I have forgotten my name!" He quickly turned around and asked God, "I'm sorry, I don't remember my name." "You're called a donkey!" God reminded him. "Thank you so much!" said the donkey warmly and turned to leave when he realised that he had forgotten his name again! "Aaaa…I'm sorry…could you please say that again?" he requested God. God was busy creating the squirrel and was furious at being disturbed again. He pulled the donkey's ears hard and yelled, "Donkey! Donkey! Donkey!" Immediately, the donkey's ears grew longer and longer till God stopped saying his name. You bet the donkey never ever forgot his name again.

08 The Feast

There lived a greedy lion king in the forest. He ate up all the food and hardly left anything for the other animals. One day, he decided to throw a grand feast at his castle. "You must all keep a nickname, only then will you be allowed to enter the castle," announced the lion. As soon as the lion left, the wise old turtle cried, "I have a plan," and winked at the other animals. On the day of the feast, all the animals went to the lion's castle. At the entrance, when the lion asked the turtle for his nickname, the turtle replied, "I am All of You," and was allowed to enter the castle. When the food arrived, the turtle stopped the server and asked, "Who is this food for?" "It's for All of You," replied the server. "Thank you," said the turtle and quickly collected all the food in a bag and went home. All the other animals followed him and enjoyed their grand feast that day.

09 The Monkey and the Jackal

Once there lived a wicked monkey who troubled the animals of the jungle. A clever jackal decided to teach him a lesson. He told the monkey, "You have a beautiful body but your ugly red face spoils your beauty. I know how to make your face handsome." The monkey was very excited and begged the jackal for advice.

The jackal explained, "When you see an elephant passing by, hit him on his forehead with a stone. What will flow down to the trunk is a magical potion. If you rub a few drops of this potion on your face, you will become the most handsome animal on Earth." The foolish monkey tried to do just that. The furious elephant caught the monkey in his trunk, whirled him round and finally, threw him to the ground with great force. The monkey was bruised all over and realised his mistake. He promised never ever to trouble the other animals again.

10 The Foxy Rooster

Once upon a time, there was a fox that lived in the wild forests of Africa. One day, the fox quietly entered a farmyard and stole a big, fat rooster. When the farmer saw the fox running away with the rooster, he raised an alarm and at once, he and his dogs started chasing him. The fox was running as fast as he could, even though he had the rooster in his mouth. "Grab that sly fox," shouted the farmer to his dogs. The rooster screamed on seeing the farmer, "Go away. I don't want to go back with you." Then the rooster told the fox that he disliked the farmer. The fox was glad to hear this and said to the farmer, "The rooster does not want to come back to you, so don't waste your time." No sooner had the fox opened his mouth, the rooster flew away and sat on a tree till his master rescued him.

11 The Crafty Crane and the Crab

Once a wily old crane thought of a plan to catch prey easily. He saw a crab passing by. "Boo hoo… boo hoo.." wept the crane. "Oh dear! What happened? Why are you crying?" asked the crab. The crane shed a few tears and said, "O' Crabby! Haven't you heard? It's not going to rain for the next twelve years. All the lakes will dry up. We will all die. I wonder what will happen to you and the fish?" When the other crabs and fish heard this, they all went to the crane for advice. The crane volunteered to take them to a nearby lake. "Don't worry, that lake will never dry up," he assured the crabs. Every day, he carried one fish away and ate it on the way. One day, it was Crabby's turn. The crab happily sat on the crane's back. After some time, Crabby saw that the path was strewn with the bones of fish and there was no lake to be seen for miles. He realised the crane's treachery. He clawed the crane's neck so hard, that the crane fell down. The clever crab ran and hid behind the rocks to save his life.

12 The Naughty Rabbit

A rabbit drank water from a river every day. But he had a big problem. Two snakes also lived in the same river. While one snake lived on the upper bend of the bank, the other lived towards the lower bend. The rabbit realised that that neither of the snakes knew about the other. "He-he-he-he! I am going to have some fun now!" thought the naughty rabbit.

He went to both the snakes separately and said, "I know you are mightier than me. But if I manage to pull you out of the water, will you let me drink water from the river?" The snakes laughed and accepted the challenge wondering how a little rabbit could possibly pull them out. Finally, the day of the challenge arrived and the rabbit placed a big grapevine near the bend. He asked both the snakes to pull hard. The snakes kept pulling the grapevine with all their might from the two ends, while the naughty little rabbit rolled on the ground and laughed till his stomach ached.

13 Reggie the Rabbit

A magician had a rabbit called Reggie. The rabbit could hide himself so well in the magician's hat that when the magician pulled him out of it, it seemed like magic. But Reggie knew that it was just a trick and not magic. He wished to be a real magic rabbit. One fine day, Reggie met a witch and asked, "Can you help me? I'm a magic rabbit but one clever boy has already found out my secret. Please make me a real magic rabbit." She agreed to help him. In the evening, at the children's party, Reggie performed his usual trick. The boy yawned, "It's the same old boring trick." Just then, Reggie grew bigger and bigger till he was the size of the monster. The children gave a cry of fright and ran here and there shouting, "Oh! That's a monster rabbit!" Reggie said to the children, "Don't be afraid, dear children. I'm not a monster." And he shrank back to his normal size. The children were delighted to see a 'talking rabbit.'

14 The Nosy Giraffe

Once, there lived a giraffe named Gerald. Because of his long neck, he could see everyone around and hear their conversation. Then he would gossip about what he'd seen and heard. It became his favourite pastime. Nothing could ever remain a secret with Gerald. The other animals were unhappy with his behaviour. One day, Gerald, as usual, bent his head to see what was happening in the Parrot House. There was some commotion going on inside and Gerald listened to everything carefully. But, he did not find it interesting. "Parrots are too noisy," he thought. When he tried to pull his neck back, he found that his neck had got stuck. Gerald felt very embarrassed. All the other animals laughed at him and said, "This is your punishment for gossiping too much." The zoo vet felt very sympathetic towards the giraffe and he helped Gerald pull out his neck. Gerald learned not to gossip and even if he heard something interesting, he kept quiet about it.

15 The Lonely Monkey

Ben the monkey felt very lonely because there was no one to play with. He lived in a tiny island in the sea. Once, a fish asked him, "Why don't you go to the island nearby? There are lots of animals there with whom you can make friends."

"I don't like to get wet!" cried Ben. "Then I will teach you to fly!" said a pelican who was flying past. But Ben couldn't learn to fly. "I will make a raft out of some trees here," said Ben. "That's silly," grumbled a turtle who was swimming nearby. "If you cut all the trees, we wouldn't have any food left on this island!" The turtle then offered him to take him to the island on his back. At the island, Ben made many new friends. He would never be lonely again!

16 Max the Circus Lion

Once upon a time, there was a circus lion called Max. Though he looked big and ferocious, he was very gentle. His trainer, Jimmy Bravo, could even put his hand inside Max's mouth without any fear. But sometimes, Max wished he could get out of his cage and roam in the jungle like other lions. One day, Jimmy accidentally left the cage open. Max quietly crept out of the cage and went to the woods. He was happy to be free and roared in happiness. A family was enjoying a picnic there. On seeing Max and hearing his roar, they were terrified. They left the food spread out on the ground and ran away. Max was sad because he wanted to make friends with those people. He ate the food lying there and then dozed off. He was woken up by the sound of sirens and was delighted to see Jimmy. "Come, Max, now you will not stay in a cage. We are going to a safari park," said the kind-hearted Jimmy. And from that day onwards, Max lived a free life and enjoyed himself.

17 Who has the Sweetest Flesh on Earth?

Long, long ago, the devil was thrown out of Heaven. He met a snake and said, "If you take me to Heaven, I will tell you who has the sweetest flesh on Earth." The snake agreed and took him to Heaven. As promised, the devil told the snake that man has got the sweetest flesh on Earth. A swallow that was present went to the snake and said, "Do you think the devil was true to you? I think we should first check if what he has told you is true." The snake agreed and a mosquito was sent to Earth to find out if the sweetest flesh on Earth is man's. After a year, the mosquito returned and told the swallow that the fact was true. The swallow bit the mosquito's tongue to prevent the truth from being known. Now, the mosquito can only buzz. The snake thought that the mosquito's buzz meant that the frog's flesh was sweetest. And from that day onwards, snakes eat frogs and mosquitoes buzz.

18 The Grateful Ant

Once, Ancy the ant was delighted to find a huge room full of grains. "Now, I will eat till my tummy bursts!" said Ancy joyfully. Ancy ate and ate until her tummy was about to burst and then she felt thirsty. She looked around for water but could find none. "If I don't get a drop of water now, I will die!" cried Ancy. Plop! A drop of water fell near the ant just then. She drank it and looked up to see where the drop had come from. She found a little girl crying. She asked the girl, "Why are you weeping, little girl?" The girl explained that a giant had locked her in the room. "He will only let me go if I separate the wheat, barley and rye from this huge heap of grains! If I cannot finish this task in a day, he will eat me up!" The ant called all her friends. Thousands of ants worked all night and made three different heaps of wheat, barley and rye. The next day, when the giant came into the room and found his work done, he set the girl free. Ancy and the little girl remained friends forever.

19 The Jackal and the Drum

One morning a jackal was walking through the forest. Drrm! Drrm! Drrrm! He heard a strange deafening sound echoing though the forest. "The hunters! The hunters have arrived!" thought the jackal in terror. He ran towards his cave and hid inside it. The jackal waited for the strange noise to go but it went on and on. The jackal's curiosity got the better of him and he decided to go and look outside. He nervously crept out of his cave and inched towards the source of the sound. He arrived near a cave and found a big drum. "There is nobody here, so how is this drum beating on its own!" thought the jackal. He peered into the drum and lo! Inside the drum was a group of little lion cubs. They were merrily dancing and beating the drum. "Oh, foolish me!" thought the jackal. "Without knowing the cause I was so terrified of this sound."

20 The Talent Contest

One day, all the animals of the jungle decided to hold a talent contest to decide who was the most useful animal. The monkey said, "I know how to swing from one tree to the other and can also throw a pair of coconuts far apart." "Oh, that sounds dangerous and harmful. You can't be useful to anyone," said the zebra, who was the judge. "Sir, I can throw a huge amount of water very far," said the elephant proudly. But the elephant was disqualified since everyone got wet when he did so. The gazelle and the tiger were also not able to impress the judge. Just then it started raining heavily and everyone started running to find shelter for themselves. Suddenly, the wooden bridge over the river broke. The crocodile said to the animals, "Don't worry, sit on my back. I'll take you all to the other side of the river." Soon all the animals climbed on the crocodile's back and reached the other side of the river. The crocodile was declared the most useful of all animals for his timely help.

21 The Flying Mail

Bertie Badger was the forest postman. Everyday, he would walk long distances through the forest to deliver letters to all the animals. The animals were very excited to see him. One day, Bertie was resting on a log and having tea after a hard day's work. A pigeon flew up to him and said, "Uncle Bertie, can I help you in delivering letters?" Bertie Badger smiled and gave a small bite of the sandwich to the pigeon. "You're too tiny to be a postman." The pigeon flew off and soon returned with a few friends. They started taking out the letters from Bertie's sack and gathered them together. The smaller birds took the mail and the bigger birds picked up the parcels. Bertie was amazed to see this. So, every day the birds would come to Bertie and help him deliver the letters. In return, Bertie gave them sandwiches every day.

22 A Snake called Crawly

Once upon a time there lived a snake called Crawly, who had no legs. So she slithered her way through fields, bushes and up the tree branches. One day all the animals in the forest decided to organise a race to crown the fastest animal. "I am the fastest animal," claimed the cheetah. "But I have the longest legs," asserted the ostrich. "I have sturdy legs," snapped the elephant.

Crawly was very upset. She went to meet her friend, the centipede and cried, "I do not have legs so I cannot participate in the race." "Of course, you can!" answered the centipede. "You see, God has given each animal a unique feature. The monkey can swing, horses gallop and birds fly." "But they all have legs!" protested Crawly. "Look at me," pointed the centipede. "Even I can't run or fly, but I can crawl." The next day Crawly slithered as fast as she could and lo! He left all the animals behind!

23 The Partridge's Nest

Once upon a time, there lived two partridges in a cornfield. One day, two tomcats captured the female partridge, who was sitting on the eggs in her nest. The older tomcat said to the younger one, "I will take the partridge since I saw her first and you keep the eggs. In any case, the eggs are of the same worth as the partridge so it should not make any difference to you." The younger one replied, "Why don't you give me the partridge and keep the eggs yourself?" Thus, they began to argue and fight with each other. In the process, the partridge was left loose and she flew away. The eggs too fell down from the younger tomcat's grip and broke. And so both the tomcats got nothing in the end.

24   Pinky Elephant's Party

Pinky Elephant, who lived in house number 13, was new to Toy Town. She decided to throw a party to make some friends. Pinky dropped an invitation card at every letterbox in the lane. When she returned, Pinky found the gate numbers of her house had fallen off. So she placed them back and closed the gate. The next day, Pinky decorated her house and cooked delicious dishes. Soon, it was four in the evening but not a single toy had come for the party. To her surprise, there were many toys passing by Pinky's house with presents in their hands! "Where are you going?" she asked them. "We are going to Pinky's party!" they replied. Suddenly, Pinky realised that she had put the numbers on her gate the wrong way. The invitation said house number 13 but the numbers on the gate read 31! Seeing this, everyone laughed and came to the party. Now, Pinky had a lot of new friends.

25   The Green Horse

Once there lived a horse named Harry who loved to watch television. One day, he saw a commercial about a hair tonic to treat balding. That day when Harry combed his hair, he was appalled to see the comb full of his hair. "Oh! I am getting bald!" cried Harry. The next day, when Harry was watching television, he saw his owner Mr. Harvey with a bottle. "It must be the hair tonic!" he thought. Harry managed to get the bottle from Mr Harvey's room. He poured the tonic into a water can, dipped himself in it and rubbed the solution all over his body. Mr. Harvey shrieked when he saw Harry, for he had turned all green. The other horses also gathered around and rolled with laughter at the comical sight. And from that day, Harry was called the 'green horse.'

26 A Bunny in the Barley

Once, Mother Bunny and her little rabbits were sitting in their burrow. She said to her children, "From today onwards, you can't run about in the corn field as Farmer Brown will be coming to cut corn." In the evening, the rabbits decided to play hide-and-seek. One of the rabbits hopped along to the cornfield and hid there. No one was able to find him and after some time, he fell asleep. After an hour, the rabbit heard a dog growling and woke up. He was terrified as the dog was about eat him up. Just then a little boy ran up to him. "Hush!" cried the boy to scare the dog. The dog ran away and the boy took the rabbit back to his burrow. Mother Bunny cried in joy to see him back, "You are a very lucky rabbit." The little rabbit learnt a lesson and didn't go to the cornfield until it was cut.

27 Jupiter and the Monkey

Once, God Jupiter decided to hold a function in the forest to judge which animal had the best looking offspring. So one by one, all the animals entered with their children. The bear said to the fox, "Aren't my babies the prettiest of all?" The fox quickly pointed out that the bear had no chance of winning the prize since there were many other prettier babies. Just then, a monkey came with her son who was flat-nosed, hairless and had crooked feet. The other animals seated in the hall gave out a contemptuous laugh at the sight of the ugly monkey kid. At once, the Mama Monkey said in a convincing tone, "It doesn't matter to me whether Jupiter rewards my son, but in my eyes, my son is the most beautiful and dearest of all." Pleased with her reply, Jupiter handed over the reward to the monkey and her baby.

28 The Story of Two Pandas

Once, there lived in China two giant pandas, called Kang and Tang. They were cousins but they disliked each other. They were always fighting over a bamboo plant, which had delicious shoots. All day, they would sit beside the plant and prevent each other from eating the shoots. One day, Kang threatened Tang, "If you don't leave this place, I'll bite your ears off!" "And I'll bite your nose!" snarled Tang. They broke into a fight, rolling over each other and trying to grab the plant. In the process, the bamboo plant broke into two but the pandas continued to fight. Meanwhile, some smaller pandas hurriedly ate the bamboo shoots. When the two cousins gave up their fight and looked around, they realised how foolish they had been. They decided to be friends and share the bamboo shoots from then on.

29 The Impatient Fawn

Freddy was an impatient fawn. He just couldn't wait to have horns like his parents. One day, he pulled out a big, forked branch from a tree and tied it on his head. "I look like my father now," Freddy said joyfully. But after some time, he just could not bear the weight of the branch on his little head and took it off. "I will wait to grow up and have horns," he said realising his folly.

30 The Simple Owl

Mr. and Mrs. Owl were disappointed to see Ron's report card. They scolded him, "Shame on you, Ron. You are at the bottom of the class. This is the first time that we have such a foolish owl in our family." Although Ron was not good at studies, he was good at catching mice. But no one appreciated Ron for this talent. Mr. Owl would give advice to other animals and in return they gave him food. One day, Mr. Owl lost his voice and he could no longer give advice to others. His supply of food was thus stopped. Ron thought this was his chance to do something for his family. He returned home in the evening after catching a dozen mice, much to the surprise of his family. Now they realised how smart Ron actually was. Mr. Owl said, "Son, now I know everyone is special in his or her own way."

Contents

The Story of the Month: Kirsi the Little Lost Lamb

The Story of the Month

Kirsi the Little Lost Lamb

01 Kirsi the Little Lost Lamb

Kirsi was a little lamb. One day, while she was out in the fields with her herd and the shepherds, something amazing happened. A shower of light spread on Earth and a million stars glimmered. Then a voice beamed from the clouds, "The son of God has been born in Bethlehem!" The shepherds cried out, "Oh! Our savoir has been born!" and immediately set out for Bethlehem. Kirsi also wanted to see this child of God. So she quietly crept out of the herd and followed in the shepherd's footsteps. However, after sometime, she lost her way and came to a forest. There she saw a hungry wolf, who commanded her to surrender. "I shall have you for dinner," howled the wolf. "Please let me go now, for I have to see the child of the Lord, in Bethlehem. I promise you that I will surrender on my way back." Kirsi earnestly asked. "Are you not scared?" asked the wolf. "The Lord will protect me," replied the lamb bravely. The wolf was stunned by the little lamb's courage. "You can go to Bethlehem, Little Lamb, for God will protect fearless lambs like you," said the ashamed wolf.

Kirsi continued with her journey and reached the outskirts of a small village. Here, she met a sheepdog that was keeping a close watch on the sheep. "Have you lost your way, Little Lamb?" asked the dog. "Yes, could you kindly show me the way to Bethlehem?" "It's not safe for a little lamb to be roaming about all alone," explained the dog. "But I must see the child of the Lord!" protested Kirsi. "Yes, I know the way to Bethlehem, but who is this child of God?" asked the curious dog. "He will save all of mankind," explained Kirsi. "Oh, that's amazing!"

exclaimed the sheepdog and showed Kirsi the way to Bethlehem. "It's across the hills and vales, where the star is shining brightest today," said the dog. Kirsi thanked him and resumed her journey. Right then, a great storm swept across the valley, clouds thundered and it began to rain heavily. Kirsi quickly found a cave and waited there patiently. "I hope I can reach Bethlehem today," she thought. After a few hours when the rains stopped, Kirsi came out and saw that the valley was flooded. She braved the gushing waters and crossed the valley. After walking for hours, she saw the brightest star in the sky and knew that she had reached Bethlehem!

The town was quiet. Kirsi crossed a number of houses and then came to a stable. She quietly moved closer to it and found Mary and Joseph admiring their newborn baby, Jesus! "Oh, there's a little lamb," cried Joseph. "Come here and see what God has given us, Little Lamb!" said Mary. Kirsi moved in closer and saw baby Jesus, who was looking like an angel. Wrapped in a soft cloth, the infant was lying peacefully. "Thank you, God, for giving me the chance to see this beautiful child!" cried Kirsi. Just then, all the shepherds who had set out to see the infant also reached. They surrounded him and praised the Lord for sending their saviour. "We are blessed to see the saviour of mankind," they said. Suddenly, one of them saw Kirsi sitting near Jesus and said, "Oh look, that's Kirsi, our lamb! What are you doing here, Kirsi? How did you know the way?" they enquired. "I was lost but God showed me the way," replied the little lamb. Everybody was surprised to hear Kirsi's tale and praised the little lamb for his bravery.

02 The Generous Camel

One day in an Arabian city called Tamul, the Earth trembled and heaved and out came a huge camel! It measured seven hundred paces. All the people of Tamul were wonder-struck. A little later, the camel gave birth to a baby camel and both the mother and the baby went to live in the mountains. The mother camel would come down from the mountains every day and give milk to the city people who gave her water, in return. Days passed and nobody in Tamul was hungry any longer. But the goat herdsmen became jealous. They said, "Nobody buys any milk from us now." Even the gardeners were not happy, as they did not have enough water to feed their plants. Both the groups together chased the camel away. From that day onwards, it is said that in the city of Tamul some people had milk and some didn't.

03 How the Rhinoceros Got His Skin

Once upon a time, in a faraway land lived a man who baked delicious cakes. One morning, a big rhinoceros approached the man. The man's heart skipped a beat seeing the ferocious animal. He had a curved horn on his nose, beady eyes and unwrinkled skin. The hungry animal asked the man for some cake. When the man refused, the rhinoceros charged at him. The man ran up a tree and waited patiently for the rhinoceros to leave. As the day progressed and temperature soared, the rhinoceros left to bathe in the sea. There he took off his skin and kept it on the beach. Meanwhile, the man was furious to see the destruction the animal had caused. He decided to teach him a lesson. He went to the beach with a bagful of breadcrumbs. The man spread sand and breadcrumbs on the rhino's skin. Then he climbed a nearby tree to watch the fun. The rhinoceros emerged from the water and wore his skin. As soon as he did, he jumped up, rolled on the sand and began scratching his skin. "My skin is itching!" he screamed. He rubbed it so violently that his smooth skin creased, formed folds and remained so forever.

04 The Pig and His Way of Life

Bonny the pig lived like any other pig in his farm pen. He always ate leftovers and slept in the muddy pool. He was happy with his life but for the taunts of Gillie the cow. She always said, "Why you dirty little pig! Why do you always have to eat leftovers and sleep in such a muddy pool?" One day, Bonny could not take it anymore and went to the judge. "Sir, Gillie always mocks me! I want your help in changing my lifestyle. I also want to eat good food like grains and peas. I want to sleep in a clean place with silk sheets under me." The judge agreed and ordered all the animals of the farm to bring peas and silk bed sheets for Bonny. He was happy and ran home to tell his wife. But Gillie's words were stuck in his mind and so when Bonny's wife asked what the judge had decided, he said, "From today onwards, we will dine on leftovers and sleep on muck!"

05 The Thieves and the Cock

Once in a village there lived a group of thieves. They were very notorious and stole money, clothes and other possessions of the village people. The villagers dreaded them but were unable to trap them or stop them from stealing. One night, the thieves entered a house of the neighbouring village. To their amazement, they were not able to find a single article which they could steal. In the end, they saw a cock which they carried away. "What do we do with this cock?" asked one of the thieves. The others replied, "Let us kill this cock." But the cock screamed, "Please don't kill me, I can be useful to you. I can wake all of you at night." The clever thief replied, "Now it is all the more necessary to kill you because you can wake up our enemies too." But before the thief could take out his knife, the cock fluttered his wings and flew away.

06 The Physician's Revenge

One day, in a great forest fire, all the animals were badly injured. The king became very concerned and asked his physician to come and treat the animals.

The physician set out for the king's court and on the way sat down under a tree to take some rest. Suddenly, a flock of crows spattered him with their droppings. The physician was furious and cursed the crows. At the court when the king asked him about the remedy for burns, the physician, who was in a bad mood and wanted to take revenge replied, "You should treat them with crow fat." The king immediately ordered the slaughter of crows to extract their fat. One by one, many crows were killed. Alarmed, the king of the crows went to meet the king. "Oh king, have mercy on the crows for we do not have any fat in our body, or else you would have already got buckets full of fat by now." The king realised his mistake. He immediately sentenced the physician to a long exile.

07 The Cat and the Hens

Once upon a time, there was a cat named Bosky. Every day he visited the farm in the hope that he could catch at least one chicken. But he never got lucky enough.

One day, as usual, Bosky was strolling past the farm. He heard Cedric the pig saying, "Oh, I am sorry to hear this! I wish, you all are well soon. Then we can play again." Bosky was excited. "Aha! The chickens are sick. I will go there as a doctor," he thought. The next day, Bosky dressed himself as a doctor and knocked at the chicken coop. "My friends, I heard that you are unwell. I have medicine for you." The chickens knew who Bosky was and they all yelled back, "Thank you, we will be fine once you go away!" Bosky left the barn, sulking at his failure once again.

08   The Cruel Master

Once in a village there lived a man. He was very cruel towards the two animals he had—a donkey and a dog. The donkey and the dog were good friends.

One night, the two animals were fast asleep in the barn. Suddenly, the dog heard a noise from outside. He nudged the donkey awake. "Wake up, my friend. There are thieves outside." "We must warn our master, otherwise, they will steal things from our house," said the donkey. The dog replied, "Dear friend, I warn you, do not wake the master. He would not appreciate your act." But the donkey did not heed his advice and brayed loudly. The thieves ran away, but the master woke up. Annoyed at being woken up in the night, he gave the donkey a good beating. The sad dog consoled his friend, "That is why I was telling you not to wake up the master."

09   The Wolves and the Sheepdogs

On the mountain, lived a pack of clever wolves. They were always on a lookout to attack the grazing sheep of the neighbouring village. But the sheep were well guarded by the sheepdogs. One day, the leader of the pack gathered all wolves and said, "Let's try to fool the sheepdogs so that we can get them out of our way." One of the wolves befriended the sheepdogs. One day he said to them, "You all are fools to serve man like this. You guard their sheep and in return you get whips and kicks from them. Come with us to our den and live with us. Both of us then can divide the meat of the sheep amongst us." The sheepdogs were fooled by the wolf's sweet talk. All of them left the flock and went to the wolf's den. As they entered all the wolves attacked and they were torn to pieces. The wolves then made a meal of the sheep.

December

10 The Good-Natured Cheetah

One day, God decided to hold a race amongst all the animals on Earth to see who was the fastest runner of all. The cheetah and the reindeer reached the semi-finals defeating everyone else. It was decided that for the semi-finals, the race would begin from a tall oak tree and end on the other side of the hill. God came down from Heaven to be the judge. Both the cheetah and the reindeer raced over levelled land and past rocky ground. The reindeer ran ahead but a little later bumped into a rock and broke his foot. He thought that he would lose. On seeing the reindeer in pain, the good-natured cheetah stopped and carried the reindeer back to the place where the race had started. God was deeply moved by the cheetah's kindness and he declared the cheetah the fastest runner on earth.

11 Mitsy's Freedom

Mitsy was a lovely green parrot that lived in a cage in Rob's house. Everyday, Rob would talk to him before leaving for school. Sometimes, Mitsy looked above at the sky and watched the other birds flying freely. "They are so lucky," he would sadly wonder. One day, Rob heard his teacher saying, "It is a crime to make anyone your slave. Without freedom, we cannot progress. It's a sin even to put animals in a cage. They too crave for freedom like us." That evening, Rob was in a thoughtful mood all the time. The teacher's words kept ringing in his ears and he thought of Mitsy. "I have committed a crime by snatching Mitsy's freedom. After all, his real place belongs in the sky like other birds, not inside a cage," realised Rob. And the next morning, before leaving for school, he opened the cage and freed Mitsy into the vast open sky.

12 Kit the Otter

Kit, a young otter, lived with his parents under the sea. He used to hide himself behind a thick bush of weeds to protect himself from the wild sea animals. He called this thick bush of weeds his 'secret place.' One morning, he heard three loud whistles. Three whistles meant danger, while a single one signalled that all was clear. His mother told him that his younger brother, who went for a swim in the sea, was chased by the huntsmen and their dogs. "I will save him," said Kit and dived into the sea. The dogs splashed into the water behind him. He found his brother and dragged him to his 'secret place'. There they hid till they heard Father Otter's single whistle. The two swam back and the otter family was reunited.

13 The Mouse Who Liked Music

Morgan was a very quiet mouse. One day, he heard some wonderful music being played in the garden. He crept out of his burrow and found a band of animals playing catchy tunes on their instruments. He wondered, "I've been so quiet all my life, maybe I should try making some noise." Morgan asked the bandleader, Snuff the dog, if he could join them. As soon as Snuff agreed, Morgan grabbed the guitar and plucked its strings so hard that they snapped. He then blew the trumpet so loud that a gush of wind came out, instead of a sound. Next, he tried the drums and beat them so hard that the noise deafened the entire band. This way Morgan took one instrument after another and created a chaos. Snuff shouted, "Q U I E T!" He snatched the instruments from Morgan and said, "You can never become a musical mouse," and walked away with the band.

14 The Lion in Love

Once there lived a ferocious lion. One day, while roaming about in the forest, the lion saw a woodcutter and his lovely young daughter, gathering wood. The lion fell in love with the beautiful girl. He growled, "Mr. Woodcutter! I want to marry your daughter!" The woodcutter became very frightened. He did not want to marry his beloved daughter to this beast, but he was also afraid to refuse the lion. So the woodcutter and his daughter thought of a plan to get rid of the lion. The woodcutter told the lion, "I will give you my daughter's hand in marriage if only you would cut you claws and pull out your teeth. They are so scary!" The foolish lion, on hearing this, agreed to do so and come again. The next day, the lion arrived toothless and clawless. This time, the woodcutter and his daughter were not scared of the beast. They drove away the foolish lion with a big club!

15 The Wolf Who Wanted to be Village Head

Once, while roaming in the forest a wolf suddenly saw an ass in the distance. "I can have that ass for lunch!" he thought and ran towards him. Seeing the wolf approaching him, the ass quickly hit upon a plan. He quietly knelt down and said, "My Lord, the village needs a brave headman like you. Will you be kind enough to accept the position?" The greedy wolf was delighted. "Sure, I will," he said. "But how can I allow you to walk all the distance, my master! Please climb on my back," requested the ass. The wolf promptly climbed up on the ass's back and was carried to the village. As soon as the ass reached the village, he started braying loudly, "Help, help, the wolf is eating me up!" The villagers came out with sticks and beat up the silly wolf!

16 Hannah's Big Day

A large colony of hedgehogs lived in a big meadow. Once in a year, all the hedgehogs used to parade and gather to celebrate the Flower Day with their favourite flower in hand. Hannah was a sweet little hedgehog. Never before in her life had she paraded. But this year she would be participating. It was a big day for her. Finally, it was time for her to choose a flower. "Mama, what do I do? I like them all. I like roses, the red poppies and the daffodils too. What should I do?" she asked. Then came along her father. He saw Hannah's confusion and told her to close her eyes and pick any one. So, Hannah picked a sunflower. In the afternoon, Hannah paraded with the sunflower. She was the happiest because she had found her favourite flower.

17 Poor Timmy

Once, there was a very fat squirrel called Timmy. He lived with his wife, Goody. Timmy loved eating nuts. Every year, before winter set in, Timmy and Goody collected bags full of nuts. One early morning, they set out to find some nuts. But when they reached the orchard, Timmy found a flock of birds eating his favourite hazelnuts. "These birds will finish all the nuts," he quipped. "Let's chase them away," said Goody and started climbing the tree. Timmy, being fat, was a very slow climber. He struggled to move faster but could not. The birds laughed and gleefully relished the nuts. Meanwhile, Goody noticed a shorter route. It was a very narrow gap, which would lead them to the birds in half the time. She quickly glided through the opening. "Hurry, the last bunch of hazelnuts are about to finish," she told Timmy. Timmy rushed into the narrow gap. "Ouch! I am stuck in the gap," he squeaked. While Timmy struggled to come out of the gap, the birds ate up the last bunch of hazelnuts and there were none for fat Timmy!

18 The Tale of Peter Rabbit

Flopsy, Mopsy, Popsy and Peter were four little rabbits. They lived with their mother next to a big cabbage garden. One day, their mother said, "I will be out for a while, none of you should go into that cabbage garden." Flopsy, Mopsy and Popsy decided to stay in the burrow. Peter, the adventurous one, peeked out of the burrow and thought, "I should try those lovely cabbages!" He sneaked into the field and began nibbling one. Suddenly, he saw a huge figure appear before him. It was Mr. McGregor, the owner of the garden. He had a large plough in his hand. "How dare you sneak into my garden and eat the cabbages?" he roared. Wasting no time, Peter turned around and darted away towards a shed. Mr. McGregor dashed behind, "I will kill you!" Terribly frightened, Peter suddenly jumped up and landed in a can of water. He knew this was the best place to hide. He held his breath, while Mr. McGregor searched everywhere. Unable to find Peter, he went away. Peter pushed his head out of the water gasping. "I almost died in there!" sighed Peter. He struggled out of the can and raced back to his burrow, relieved to be alive.

19 Uncle Spider

Anansi was a clever spider. One day, he went to the hyena's cave and sat beside the cubs. He told them, "I am your Uncle. My name is For-You-All. If your mother brings food for me let me know." Saying this, he went to a corner. Mother Hyena came with meat and said, "Come kids! The meat is for you all!" The kids gave away the food to the spider. In the evening, when the mother came, the kids asked for more food. They also told her about the spider. The mother was very angry and chased the spider. Anansi ran to the dog's cave and when the hyena came, he said that it was the dog who ate her food. The hyena now chased the dog and Anansi saved himself.

20   The Ant and the Chrysalis

Once, an ant was running about on the lawn when he happened to see a chrysalis, which was going through a phase change. The ant went near chrysalis and said, "I feel sorry for you. You can hardly move about. Look at me! I can reach wherever I want. My life is much better than yours!" The chrysalis heard everything quietly but did not say anything. The ant grinned and went away. A few days later, the ant went to see the chrysalis again. But on reaching there, all he saw was a shell. The ant was wondering what could have happened to the shell when suddenly, he felt something fluttering above his head. He looked up and saw a pretty, colourful butterfly. "You pitied me, my friend. Try following me now and we'll see who's better off," challenged the butterfly. Saying so, the butterfly rose higher and soon flew out of sight. The ant was left speechless this time. Appearances can be deceptive.

21   The Fox and the Turtle

Once, there was a fox, who had been searching for food for a very long time. At last, he reached a river and caught a turtle. The fox greedily tried to take a bite of the turtle but could not break through its hard shell. The fox was wondering what to do when the shrewd turtle suggested, "Why don't you put me in the water for some time? Then my body will become soft and spongy and you'll easily be able to eat me up."

The fox thought it was a good idea and dipped the turtle in the river. The turtle had just been waiting for this opportunity. He quickly swam to the mid point of the river and laughed, "I'm cleverer than you. Now you'll remain hungry."

22 The Greedy Sparrow

Some birds used to live together in a tree in the forest. There was a wise bird amongst them whom the other birds addressed as King Bird. Once, when it was extremely hot, the King Bird advised all the birds to fly to a valley near the Himalayas. Trusting their king, all the birds found a cooler home near the mountains and lived comfortably. There was a greedy sparrow in this flock of birds. One day, she noticed a cart carrying grains to the king's palace. She hopped down on the grains and ate to her heart's content. But, she advised the other birds that they should keep away from the road as the cart could kill them. The next day, the sparrow saw the same cart and started eating the grain. As the sparrow was doing so, a big vulture grabbed her and ate her. When King Bird heard of the incident, he said, "Those who advise others with an evil and selfish intention, will suffer."

23 The Lion, the Bear and the Fox

Once a lion and a bear lived in a forest. One day, they happened to grab a kid. But, after some time they started fighting over who would take the kid and have it for dinner. Both suffered scratches and injuries. At last, when none could come out as winner, they gave up the fight and lay worn out. The smaller animals and birds waited excitedly to see who would be the winner. A fox, who had been intently watching the fight for a long time, quickly came in between the two animals, grabbed the kid and ran away as fast as he could. The lion and the bear were left staring in amazement. The bear said to the lion, "Alas! We had been working so hard to get hold of that kid and the reward went to the fox, who did nothing."

24 Freddie's Cap

Once there lived two giraffes, Gertie and her baby, Freddie, in a zoo. Everyday, they would stand by their bars and people would come to have a look at them. One day, Gertie saw a group of little boys and their teacher watching them. All the boys were wearing red caps and this really fascinated Gertie. She wished that Freddie could wear the same cap. While the teacher was telling the boys about giraffes, Gertie thrust her neck outside the bars and pulled off a boy's cap. Pulling her neck back in, she placed the cap on Freddie's head. The little boy, whose cap Gertie had taken, began to cry. The zookeepers tried to get back the cap from Gertie, but she would not return it. So a new cap was bought for the little boy and Freddie wore the red cap every day.

25 The Sly Crow

A sly crow and a cuckoo lived in the same tree. It was autumn and both the cuckoo and the crow were about to lay eggs. The crow saw that the cuckoo had built a comfortable nest and thought, "I'll lay my eggs in the cuckoo's nest and let her hatch them. My fledglings will look just like the cuckoo's." When the cuckoo went to look for food, the sly crow went and laid her eggs in the cuckoo's nest and dropped the cuckoo's eggs down. The cuckoo sat on the eggs for days and days. When they hatched, she nursed the young fledglings. The lazy crow watched from her nest. Time passed and the fledglings grew up. One morning, the cuckoo looked at her babies carefully and found that they were not cuckoos, but crows. She looked at the crow and understood what her sly neighbour had done. The cuckoo was furious and flew away to make a nest elsewhere.

26 Mitty's Surprise

"It was a bright and lovely day. Mitty the cat woke up from her sleep and stretched. Bob the bumblebee went buzzing by and shouted out to Mitty to wake up. Mitty had many friends and they all were very fond of her. "Where are my children?" Mitty asked. "I saw them having breakfast a few minutes back," said Betty. "All right, Mitty, we have work to do. We'll see you in the evening." Mitty closed her eyes and purred. She was happy with her life. She waited for her food. A six year old boy came out with a bowl of milk and bread and placed it near Mitty. Mitty meowed her thanks and ate her food. A little later, she heard Rita the robin chirping. She was Mitty's best friend. "Mitty, help me search for food," said Rita. "Oh! There are plenty of juicy wiggly worms around. I'll find some for you," said Mitty. Suddenly, they heard a loud 'ssshhh' sound echoing across the sky. "What's that?" asked Mitty. The sound grew louder. Bob too came buzzing by. "I think the clouds are falling," he said and hid under a bush. As the sound came closer, Mitty was surprised to see a huge hot air balloon floating above. It was a beautiful pink balloon with a big flower made on it. "What a wonderful sight!" said Rita, "how silly of us to be scared!" The children were running after the balloon in great excitement. Mitty was delighted at the end of the day. "What an exciting day it has been!" she said to her friends and went to take a nap.

27 The Helpful Rabbit

Bozo was a helpful rabbit and everybody loved him. One day, Bozo was resting under a tree. Suddenly a stone hit his head. Bozo looked around in alarm and saw a young boy with a catapult in the bushes nearby. Bozo sprang up and ran to warn his friends. "Be careful, I just saw someone around. He has come to kill us with stones," said Bozo. The rabbits decided to go deep into the forest and hide in the bushes. As Bozo turned around to go, he heard a mournful cry. He looked back and saw that the boy with the catapult had been stung badly by a bee. "Heeeeelp!" cried out the boy as his catapult fell from his hands. His face was red and swollen. Bozo ran to help the boy and rubbed some medicinal herbs on the sting. "Thank you," said the boy feeling very ashamed and promised never to hunt animals again.

28 Cathy's Tea Party

Once, Cathy the crab, decided to have a tea party at the bottom of the ocean. She prepared lots of iced buns, a big cake, two big plates of seaweed sandwiches and a large jar of orange juice for her guests. Cathy decorated her house with colourful balloons and ribbons. Then, she laid out eight plates and eight cups and saucers on the table. Some fish curiously watched Cathy's little house and wondered who the special guest was.

"Go away, you fish. Stop spying on others. Don't you know it's a bad habit?" she shouted at them. One fish cheekily enquired, "Cathy, it seems you'll be having a lot of guests today." Cathy giggled and said, "No, there's only one guest." Just then, Ollie the octopus swam by and said, "Those eight plates are for my eight arms," and burst out laughing.

December

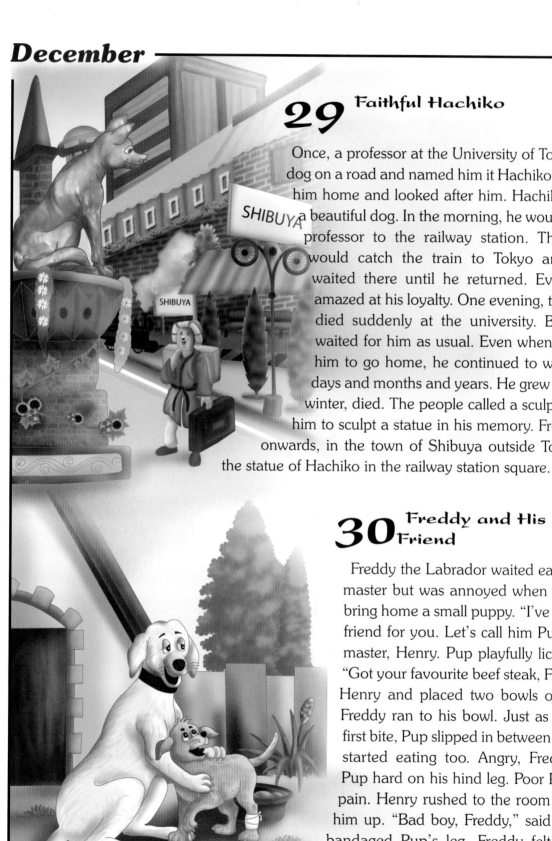

29 Faithful Hachiko

Once, a professor at the University of Tokyo found a dog on a road and named him it Hachiko. He brought him home and looked after him. Hachiko grew into a beautiful dog. In the morning, he would follow the professor to the railway station. The professor would catch the train to Tokyo and Hachiko waited there until he returned. Everyone was amazed at his loyalty. One evening, the professor died suddenly at the university. But Hachiko waited for him as usual. Even when people told him to go home, he continued to wait there for days and months and years. He grew old and one winter, died. The people called a sculptor and told him to sculpt a statue in his memory. From that day onwards, in the town of Shibuya outside Tokyo, stands the statue of Hachiko in the railway station square.

30 Freddy and His Little Friend

Freddy the Labrador waited eagerly for his master but was annoyed when he saw him bring home a small puppy. "I've got a young friend for you. Let's call him Pup," said his master, Henry. Pup playfully licked Freddy. "Got your favourite beef steak, Freddy," said Henry and placed two bowls on the floor. Freddy ran to his bowl. Just as he took his first bite, Pup slipped in between his legs and started eating too. Angry, Freddy nipped Pup hard on his hind leg. Poor Pup cried in pain. Henry rushed to the room and picked him up. "Bad boy, Freddy," said Henry and bandaged Pup's leg. Freddy felt guilty and ashamed. He nursed Pup all night. Next morning, Pup was better and Freddy gave him a big hug. "Friends!" said Freddy. Pup licked Freddy's face all over.

31 The Two Horses

Once upon a time there lived a king's horse and a peasant's horse. The king's horse had a furry mane and was of the finest breed. He really looked very magnificent. The peasant's horse, on the other hand, was not a well-bred horse and had to stay in a dirty stable. The king's stunning horse often bragged about himself. "Look at me, you dirty horse. I am one of the finest breeds, have a well-shaped body and am superior in every way. Nobody can match up to me," he boasted. To prove his point, he challenged the peasant's horse to a race and it was agreed that the one who tires out first would lose the race.

The enthusiastic king's horse began galloping immediately, while the peasant's horse only walked. "Oh, you can't even run!" mocked the king's proud horse. Saying this, he galloped even faster and completed each round swiftly. After sometime, however, he began gasping for breath and slowed down his pace. In a while, his legs ached and he limped all the way.

Meanwhile, the peasant's horse had just increased his speed. He moved on steadily and overtook the king's horse soon. "Ha! Ha! Ha! What happened, dear friend? It seems you are already tired," he jeered at the king's horse, who by now was dragging himself to remain in the race. He realised that he was going to lose the race and was very ashamed. He hung his head in shame and walked on quietly, promising never to brag again.